Mr Corbett's Ghost

A brilliant collection of three short stories from a master story-teller, who will keep you turning the pages until the very end. The chilling title story tells of a young apprentice who makes a pact with a strange old man one New Year's Eve to rid the world of Mr Corbett, his cruel employer. Sure enough, Mr Corbett meets an untimely death, but the tables turn on the terrified apprentice who finds himself cursed with the ghost of the man he hated most in the world . . .

LEON GARFIELD was born and educated in Brighton on the south coast of England. His art studies were interrupted by the Second World War, during which he served in the Army Medical Corps. After the war he worked as a hospital laboratory technician until he gave this up to devote himself to writing. He is the author of a number of highly acclaimed novels, some of which have been serialized on television and made into films, includung *Mr Corbett's Ghost* which was filmed in 1987. His books have been widely translated and have won many international and British literary awards including the Guardian Award, the Whitbread Award, and the Carnegie Medal. In 1981 he was nominated for the prestigious Hans Christian Andersen Award. He was married to the novelist Vivien Alcock and they have a daughter who is a teacher. They lived in North London, where many of his novels are set, until his death in 1996.

Leon Garfield

Mr Corbett's Ghost
and Other Stories

Illustrated by Jason Cockcroft

OXFORD
UNIVERSITY PRESS

OXFORD
UNIVERSITY PRESS

Great Clarendon Street, Oxford OX2 6DP

Oxford University Press is a department of the University of Oxford.
It furthers the University's objective of excellence in research, scholarship,
and education by publishing worldwide in

Oxford New York
Athens Auckland Bangkok Bogotá Buenos Aires Calcutta
Cape Town Chennai Dar es Salaam Delhi Florence Hong Kong Istanbul
Karachi Kuala Lumpur Madrid Melbourne Mexico City Mumbai
Nairobi Paris São Paulo Singapore Taipei Tokyo Toronto Warsaw

and associated companies in Berlin Ibadan

Oxford is a registered trade mark of Oxford University Press
in the UK and in certain other countries

First published by Longmans 1969
Published in Puffin Books 1971
Oxford edition published 1999
Reprinted 1999

British Library Cataloguing in Publication Data available

Cover illustration by Jason Cockcroft

ISBN 0 19 271810 X

Typeset by AFS Image Setters Ltd, Glasgow

Printed and bound in Great Britain by
Biddles Ltd, Guildford and King's Lynn

Contents

1
MISTER CORBETT'S GHOST

To Nancy and Edward

CHAPTER ONE

A windy night and the old year dying of an ague. Good riddance! A bad old year, with a mean spring, a poor summer, a bitter autumn—and now this cold, shivering ague. No one was sorry to see it go. Even the clouds, all in black, seemed hurrying to its burial somewhere past Hampstead.

In the apothecary's shop in Gospel Oak, the boy Partridge looked up through the window to a moon that stared fitfully back through the reflections of big bellied flasks, beakers, and retorts. Very soon now he'd be off to his friends and his home to drink and cheer the death of the old year—and pray that the new one would be better. And maybe to slip in a prayer for his master, Mister Corbett, the apothecary himself. Such a prayer!

'May you be like this year that's gone, sir, and take the same shivering ague! For your seasons weren't no better.'

He stared at the oak bench that shone with his sweat—and at the great stone mortar and pestle in which his spirit had been ground.

'May you creak and groan like your shop sign in this wild wind, sir.'

Now there passed by in the moon-striped street a pair of draper's apprentices. Friends. They grinned and waved as they went, and their lips made: 'See you later, Ben!'

He waved back. They glanced at one another, looked up and down the street and then came leaping quaintly to the shop where they fattened their noses on the window, making pinkish flowers in the glass.

Benjamin made a face. They made two, very diabolical.

'Can we come in, Ben?'

'Yes—for a moment.'

Into the strange and gloomy shop they came, with looks of cautious wickedness.

'Make a brew, Ben.'

'Make a bubbling charm.'

'Turn old Corbett into a rat or a mouse . . .'

Like the forced-up sons of witches, they had begun to caper round the great stone mortar. Glumly, Benjamin looked on, wishing he could oblige them, but not knowing how.

Huge wild shadows leaped among the retorts and crucibles, but they were the only uncanny things about . . . save in the apprentices' minds. Now they began to screech and laugh and caper more crazily than ever, so that their faces seemed to dance in the heavy air like rosy fireflies.

'Turn him into a worm!'

'Turn him into a snail!'

'Turn old Corbett into a beetle, Ben—and step on him!'

'Be quiet!' cried Benjamin of a sudden. 'He'll hear!'

The draper's apprentices grew still. The stairs at the back of the shop creaked. But then, so did every other mortal thing in that blustering night.

'Turn him into a—'

But Benjamin Partridge did not hear what other witchcraft was being asked of him. His mind was suddenly distracted: partly by listening to a further creaking of the stairs, and partly by a chill and a darkness—like a cloud across the moon—that had passed over his heart. He shivered. His two friends stared at him: then to each other. They shrugged their shoulders.

'Happy New Year, Ben.'

Then they left him for the more cheerful street. With their going, the chill within him grew curiously sharper. His back itched, as if he was being watched. He went to the window and waved his friends on their way; and in the jars that sat like short fat magistrates on the shelves, no more than a tiny waving Partridge was reflected. A drab dressed little soul of a boy seemed to struggle to get out.

Now it was half after seven o'clock. Time to be gone. He pulled his patched grey coat from under the counter and began to put it on.

'Sharp to be off, Master Partridge?'

Slippered Mister Corbett was slunk down his stairs, quiet as a waistcoated rat. Or had he been on the stairs all the time? Uneasily, Benjamin wondered what his master had heard. Mister Corbett's lips were pressed tight together. A muscle in his cheek twitched and jumped; his hands were clenched so fiercely that the blood was fled from his knuckles as if in dismay. Could he have heard?

'It—it's half after seven, Mister Corbett, sir.'

'What's half after seven when there's work to be done?'

His unpleasant eyes, swollen by spectacles, stared round the shop. 'There's dust on the bottle-tops, Master Partridge. Would you leave it so? Polish the bottles before you go.'

The apprentice sighed, but did as he was told. And Mister Corbett, pale of face and round of shoulder, watched him.

'Not willingly done, Master Partridge. Too anxious to be out and wild as a fox.'

'It's twenty to eight, Mister Corbett, sir. It's New Year's Eve—'

'What's New Year's Eve when there's work to be done? There's a smear of grease on the bench.'

Once more the apprentice sighed, but polished away at the mark that had been left by his own sweat.

'Not willingly done, Master Partridge. Your heart

wasn't in it. Still less was your soul. I want your heart and soul, Master Partridge. I expect them. I demand them.'

His eyes grew hard as he spoke and blotches came into his grey cheeks. He saw his apprentice was defiant, and would keep his heart and soul for himself.

'It's five to eight, Mister Corbett, sir. I would be home—'

'What's your home to me, Master Partridge? What's your family and friends to me when I've not got your heart and soul? For you're no use to me if I don't have all of you. There's a dribble of wet on that flask by your hand, Master Partridge. Wipe it off.'

The wetness was a fresh-fallen tear, but the apprentice scorned to say so—even though others were beginning to leak out of his bitter eyes. Eight o'clock and his friends would be waiting and his mother would be laying up a fine table . . .

The apothecary peered once more round his shop. Was there nothing else to be done? Momentarily, his eyes flickered towards his private doorway behind which dwelt his wife and children in his private world.

The boy watched him hopefully, fancied he'd glimpsed a softening . . .

'Then—' he began; but there came an urgent tapping at the window. The apothecary smiled harshly.

'A customer, Master Partridge. How lucky you're still here. Open the door for the gentleman. And wait.'

A retired lawyer's clerk, maybe—or a neglected scrivener. Very small and old and dusty, and all in black. Very wrinkled about the cheeks—as if he'd put on a skin the cat had slept on. He brought a queer smell into the shop with him, damp and heavy: an undertaker, perhaps?

Mister Corbett rubbed his hands together and showed all his teeth in a dreadful smile.

'Not shut? Still at work, eh?' muttered the old man sniffily, as if he had the beginnings of a chill.

Benjamin Partridge eyed him miserably. An old fellow like him would need a deal of medicine. And then to what purpose?

'Never too late to be of service, sir,' said the apothecary. 'Me and the apprentice. Heart and soul in our trade. No matter what the time—or the day. Heart and soul, eh, Master Partridge?'

The old man nodded briefly and seemed not to notice the furious dismay in the apprentice's face.

'This mixture, then. Very important. Want it tonight. Can you oblige?'

He gave the apothecary a paper. Mister Corbett read it. He frowned. He glanced round his shelves. Then he smiled again. (What ugly teeth he had! Like railings.)

'Pleased to oblige, sir. Will you wait?'

The old man sniffed very hard. By chance, it seemed, his curiously bright eyes caught those of the apprentice. But once more he appeared not to notice the wretchedness in them.

'Wait? On New Year's Eve? And in my state of age and health? No. Deliver it. I'll be in Jack Straw's Castle. Not too far, eh? He-he! Deliver it, man. And soon.'

With that he was gone—remarkably quick and spry for a man in his state of health—and leaving behind in the shop an unmistakable smell of graveyards.

The boy Partridge shut the door after him but was too angry and distressed to notice that he'd vanished from the street, though no sound of horse or carriage had been heard.

Back in the shop, the apothecary had begun on measuring and weighing and grinding and mixing, and his apprentice looked on with ever-mounting misery and dismay. New Year's Eve was ticking slowly and surely away.

At last it was done. The mixture was bottled and ready. Hurriedly, Benjamin cleaned and cleared away till the shop shone like a new knife.

'Was it willingly done, Master Partridge?'

'Willingly . . . willingly!' cried Benjamin desperately.

His coat was on again. He was at the door. It was half after nine, and he had a long walk home. In his wild need to be out and away he turned pleadingly to his master.

'They'll be waiting now, sir! I must be gone! Everything is clean and shining. Nothing's left undone. A . . . a happy New Year to you, sir!'

'Yes, indeed, Master Partridge,' smiled Mister Corbett. 'You're willing enough. So a happy New Year to you—'

Benjamin was in the street. His face was shining, his hopes were suddenly high again. In an hour he'd be home—

'But of course you'll deliver this mixture first, Master Partridge?'

Mister Corbett's hand held out the bottle, and Mister Corbett's eyes stared cruelly into his. Benjamin's heart turned to lead. Had it been in the apothecary's hand at that moment, even he, with all his chemical knowledge, would have pronounced it to be lead.

'B-but it's all of three mile, sir! Three dark and windy miles! It'll be the New Year afore I'm back! They're waiting on me—'

'If they love you heart and soul, Master Partridge, they'll keep on waiting—'

'But there's thieves and footpads and murderers—'

'Pooh!' declared the apothecary generously. 'What will such fellows want with a lad in a patched coat? Safe as a coach and four, Master Partridge! Believe me, poor clothes give better protection than chain mail.'

'But there's gibbets and corpses and, most likely, ghosts—'

'Then take you this extra jar, Master Partridge,' beamed

the apothecary, handing him just such an item, 'and if you should be lucky enough to meet with a spectre, phantom or ghost, then snip off a piece of it and bottle it quick. Then you and I will examine it shrewdly—and send it off to Apothecaries' Hall! Ha-ha!'

'But . . . but—' stammered Benjamin, despairing of anything else to move his master. For some strange reason, he could not come out with what troubled and disturbed him almost as much as his loss of New Year's Eve.

'But . . . but—' he struggled, and still could not say what was creeping coldly round his heart. The old man: the uncanny customer in black, who repelled him in the queerest way.

Thieves and gibbets and murderers were one thing. The dusty old man who had smelled of the grave was quite another. For when he'd come, there had passed once more, like a cloud across the moon, a darkness and a chill over Benjamin's heart. He shivered in his cracked boots.

'But . . . but what if I lose my way, sir?' he came out with at length.

'What's this?' cried the apothecary angrily, for he'd lost patience, standing out in the cold. 'Did you think I'd go, then? Or did you think I'd send Mrs Corbett or one of my own children? Is *that* what's been fermenting in your unwilling mind, Master Partridge?'

Wretchedly, Benjamin shook his head.

'Won't you . . . take pity on me, sir? On this night of all nights?'

Harshly, the apothecary stared down at his white-faced apprentice. Maybe too much chemistry had turned him to iron.

'Pity, Master Partridge? What's pity when there's work to be done? Be off with you! And if you should weary on the way, remember—it *may* be a matter of life and death. Run fast, Master Partridge. Run as if—as if *my* life depended on it!'

CHAPTER TWO

'So I'm to run as if *your* life depended on it, am I, Mister Corbett? Well . . . well, watch me, then! You just watch me as I nip up this hill.

'Lord, Mister Corbett! Was that a snail that passed me by? For shame! Who'd have thought a snail would have beaten an apprentice running as if his master's life depended on it?'

Benjamin Partridge shook his head as if surprised to discover how leadenly he was mounting up dark Highgate Hill.

'Dreadful thing! Imagine old Mister Corbett perishing in Gospel Oak. Breathing his last.

'But here comes Benjamin, a-pounding through the winter's night! See that bush ahead? If I reach it before I can count to ten, Mister Corbett'll be saved! Hurry . . . hurry!

'*Eleven!* Just too late. And after I tried! Heart and soul, Mister Corbett. Just as you'd have liked . . .'

Benjamin Partridge, now near the top of Highgate Hill, fixed his young face into a crooked smile. He'd a strong imagination and saw—in his mind's eye—the apothecary corpsed and coffined in his neat back parlour (the holy place!) with a wreath at his feet inscribed:

FROM BENJAMIN PARTRIDGE. IN RESPECTFUL MEMORY.

Then, from a distance, a clock struck ten and the apprentice listened in dismay. Such chance as he'd had of reaching his home before New Year was now almost gone.

He wavered. Looked behind him—then ahead. A curious frown flickered across his face, and he began to hurry—even to run; yet not without mumbling into his wretchedly thin coat that he was making no haste on Mister Corbett's account and that he'd sooner yield up his heart and soul to the Devil than leave them in pawn in Gospel Oak.

A coachman turning into the Gatehouse Tavern out of the creaking night, was much struck by the hurrying boy's face—which passed him patchily and then was gone on, into the cheerless dark.

'Such a mixture of anger and dismay as had no business hanging about chops so tender and young. But God send him a happy New Year, and spare him from some of this bitter wind!'

The night was now grown wilder and the wind banged and roared about the air like an invisible tiger, madly fancying his stripes to be bars. (Pray to God he don't get out!)

'Rot you, Mister Corbett! May this wind blow you to Kingdom Come! May it whistle through your skin and play its tunes on your mean old bones!'

On and on he ran (but not for Mister Corbett's sake!), now stumbling, now turning this way and that to avoid the wild passion of the night. It seemed to be striving to pluck him off the world by his coat tails, did that queer and even extraordinary wind that blew mainly from Islington, Wapping, and Tower Hill.

Seven churches with open belfries stood direct in the wind's path from Wapping: St Bride's, St Jude's, St Mary's, St Peter's, St Michael's and St Michael-on-the-Hill's. Through each of them it flew, making the black bells shift and shudder and sound unnatural hours. The very ghosts of chimes and the phantoms of departed hours. Twenty-eight o'clock gone and never to return. What a knell for the dying year!

Benjamin Partridge put his head down into his skimpy collar and hastened on faster yet. (But not as Mister

Corbett would have had him hasten. There was a darkness on his spirit quite out of the apothecary's chemistry.)

His right-hand pocket was bulky with the bottle for the queer old customer, and his left hand banged against his knee, reminding him of Mister Corbett's little joke—the empty jar for 'the piece of a ghost'.

'A piece of you, Mister Corbett—that's what I'd like in your jar! And I'd set it on me mantelshelf at home, as neatly labelled as you'd like. Apothecary's heart. Very small. Very hard. Very difficult to find.'

Now the wind came wilder yet, and it seemed—to the buffeted boy—to have a strange smell upon its breath. It smelled fishy and riverish (as became its Wapping origins) and sweetish in a penetrating kind of way.

The Lord knew where it had been or what unsavoury heads it had blown through! Heads of chained pirates drowned under three tides at Shadwell Stair, full of water fury; heads of smiling traitors, spiked on the Tower, full of double hate; heads of lurking murderers in Lamb's Conduit Fields, heads of lying attorneys, false witnesses, straw friends, iron enemies, foxes, spies, and adders . . .

A sudden screaming from Caen Wood caused Benjamin Partridge to clap his hands to his ears and fairly fly. What had it been? A committee of owls over a dead starling? Most likely . . . most likely . . .

Ahead lay a little nest of lights winkling out the dark. The Spaniards' Inn. Sounds of singing and laughter came faintly from within. A cheerful company, drinking out the dying year.

The turnpike keeper in his tiny house hard by saw the boy pause and stare towards the inn with miserable longing on his face.

Poor devil! he thought. To be out on such a night!

Then he saw the boy shake his head violently and mouth the word 'No!' several times before hurrying on into the cheerless dark.

'God send you a happy New Year!' he murmured. 'And spare you from some of this bitter wind.'

Benjamin Partridge's head had suddenly been filled with dreams of another, more cheerful company, made up of his friends and his mother: candle-lit and fire-warmed faces to the window, waiting on his coming.

Then the wind had blown out these dreams and left nothing but darkness within him.

There seemed to come over his hastening form a curious difference. His running was grown more purposeful. At times, he seemed to outpace the wind itself—bending low and rushing with an oddly formidable air. His coat tails flapped blackly, like the wings of a bird of ill omen.

'Coming for you, Mister Corbett. Coming for you!'

Already he could see the top of Hampstead Hill. On either side of him the trees bent and pointed, and high upstairs the tattered clouds flew all in the same direction. The dark wind was going to Hampstead, too, and it was in the devil of a hurry.

At last, he could see Jack Straw's Castle: a square-built, glum and lonely inn scarce half a mile ahead. Doubtless, the queer customer was sat by the parlour fire, snuffling for his mixture. Then let him snuffle till the cows came mooing home! Benjamin Partridge was on a different errand now.

He continued for maybe another thirty yards. Then he stopped. To his left lay a path, leading down into the dark of the Heath.

A curious darkness. Earlier, there had been rain and certain roots and growths had caught a phosphorescence; spots of light glimmered in the bushy nothingness.

Before, these uneasy glintings might have frightened the boy, for they were very like eyes—and malignant ones at that. But now he scarcely saw them: the dreadful wind had blown out of his head all thoughts

but hatred for the mean and pale apothecary who'd sent him forth.

He began to descend the path. The earth was wet and sobbed under his feet.

'May you sob likewise, Mister Corbett—when I'm done with you!'

For the first part of its length the path dropped pretty sharply, and soon Benjamin was out of the worst of the wind. But in its place was a wretched dampness that crept and clung about him. Likewise, there was a continual breathing rustling that seemed to inhabit the various darknesses that lay about the path.

Several times he paused, as if debating whether or not to abandon his purpose and fly back to the high road and on to the inn. This path was disquieting, and it was growing worse. But each time he seemed to see Mister Corbett's face before him, mouthing, 'Heart and soul, Master Partridge. I want 'em.' And Benjamin

Partridge went on: for hatred, though it may harden the heart, softens the brain, renders it insensible to danger, and leads it in the way of darkness, madness, and evil . . . At the end of this terrible path, there stood a terrible house.

It was a tall, even a genteel house, often glimpsed from the high road from where it looked like a huge undertaker, discreetly waiting among the trees.

What was then so terrible about it that even the whispering darkness, the crooked trees, and the crooked sky were small things beside it? The visitors it had.

Old gentlemen with ulcers of the soul for which there was no remedy but—revenge! Ruined gamblers, discredited attorneys, deceivers and leavers, treacherous soldiers, discharged hangmen, venomous servants, murderous constables . . . coming chiefly at dusk, furtively grinning for—revenge. In this grim regiment Benjamin Partridge now numbered himself.

The path grew level. One by one the glinting eyes winked shut as scrubs obscured them.

'And so may your eyes shut, Mister Corbett: just like that! Ah!'

Benjamin Partridge stopped. Before him stood the house. Three pairs of windows it had, but they were dark. An iron lantern swung in the porch making queer grunting sounds as it swung against its hook. *Ugh . . . ugh . . . ugh . . .* But the three candles within burned untroubled.

There was a lion's head knocker on the door. A good brass knocker such as might have cost five pounds in the shop by Aldgate Forge. (Or had it been cast in a deeper forge than Aldgate, even?)

The boy shivered . . . most likely from the damp. He knocked on the door. A harsh and desolate sound. Came a flap of footsteps: very quick. Then they stopped.

The boy made as if to draw back—maybe to make off, even at this late stage? *No.* He knocked again.

'Nails in your coffin, Mister Corbett.'

The door opened. The boy cried out. Candle in hand, peering out with unnaturally bright eyes, was the queer customer! He said: 'I thought you'd call here first—'

CHAPTER THREE

It was said there was a room at the top of the house where certain transactions took place. The windows of this room were sometimes pointed out, for they could be seen from the high road, staring coldly through the trees.

It was rumoured that this room, ordinary enough in all its furnishings, held an item so disagreeable that it chilled the soul. Visitors had been known to stare at it, lose their tongues, fidget, then leave in haste never to return.

Benjamin peered past the old man into the dark of the house. His eyes glanced upward. Catching this look, the old man dropped his gaze in an oddly embarrassed fashion.

'Are you—are you sure, young man?'

(Was there truly such a room? Or was it all a tale told by apprentices at dead of night?)

The old man sniffed.

'Forgive me, young man—but are you sure? I must know. We don't want to waste our time do we? You've considered? You've thought? If you change your mind now, I won't be offended. Far from it! In a way, I'll be pleased. There, young man! I see you bite your lip. So why not turn about and forget it all? I'll not say anything. All will be forgot. We've never met! Come, young man—that's what you really want, ain't it? It was all a foolish idea—the black thought of a black moment. So say no more and be gone!'

He paused and stared at his young caller with a quaintly earnest air. He took a pace down so that he and the boy stood on a level. They were of a height. Maybe, even, Benjamin was a shade the taller.

'Admit now—your heart and soul ain't in it?'

An unlucky expression! Whatever of doubt or uneasiness Benjamin might have felt (and he felt both, for he was but human) shrank beside the sudden image of skinny, grinning Mister Corbett grating, 'Heart and soul, Master Partridge. I want them. I demand them!'

'Let me in,' muttered Benjamin bleakly.

The house smelled of graveyards—as did the old man—but otherwise it was no glummer than a parlour in Bow. The old man shrugged his shoulders, as if he'd done what he could, and led the way.

'This way, young man. Tread carefully. The stairs are treacherous. I don't want your death on my hands!'

So there was such a room aloft.

Benjamin's heart began to struggle in his breast. His breath came quickly and made thin patterns in the candle light. The old man paused. He jerked the candle down, thereby causing banisters and certain respectable pieces of mahogany furniture to take fright and crouch in their own shadows.

'Remember, young man—it's heart and soul or nothing!'

Again, fear and doubt fell away as Mister Corbett's face was before Benjamin. His heart grew steady under a ballast of two years' hating.

'It's heart and soul, all right! And I'll tell you—'

'Tell me nothing!' interrupted the old man curtly. 'No reasons, *if* you please! Reasons ain't my concern. Had my fill of 'em, young man. Reasons that would freeze the ears off a brass monkey. Payment's my concern.'

Nervously Benjamin felt in his pocket. Not much there. But he hoped with all his heart and soul it was enough to procure—Mister Corbett's death!

'Nothing now,' said the old man, observing Benjamin's action and divining its result. 'I don't aim to beggar you. My terms is fairer than that. A quarter of your earnings from now till—'

'Till when?'

'Till you die, young man. Just till then. And then you're free. Paid up. Discharged. Now, no haggling *if* you please. This ain't a market-place. Take my terms or leave 'em. A quarter of everything from now till Doomsday. I always deal in quarters. Always have and always will. So it'll be fivepence out of every one and eightpence. Or, if you prosper (and please God you do!), five shillings out of every pound. No more: no less. Don't be offended, young man. I always put my terms straight. Ask anyone . . .'

But Benjamin was not disposed to ask anyone. The terms seemed reasonably fair, future payment being a cheerfuller prospect than present expense. He nodded in as businesslike a fashion as the circumstance allowed.

The old man shook his head and, with many a painful sigh, continued upward into the night.

'Another floor, young man. The top of the house.'

'I know,' said Benjamin.

Again, the old man paused. He peered down over the banister with an air of resentment, as if a confidence had been betrayed and a secret blown to the winds. He seemed to shiver before mounting the remaining stairs briskly. Benjamin followed.

'This is the room,' said the old man, and pushed open a door.

For no reason but expectation, Benjamin shrank back into his pitiful coat. Yet the room was quiet. A fire burned subtly in the grate, and the furnishings were as genteel as anything else in the house. True, there was a smell of graveyards, but no worse than in the hall downstairs.

'Come inside,' said the old man, lighting a second candle. 'Come in and sit you down.'

His voice was grown suddenly courteous, as if long custom in that room had got the better of him. 'Take a chair by the fire, dear sir.'

But Benjamin did not hear him. He was peering round for the dreadful item that was to chill him to the soul.

'The chair, sir. Take a seat. This is journey's end.'

Benjamin recollected himself, attempted to smile, then sat in a chair as ordinary as an attorney's. Likewise the desk the old man was fumbling in, and a sideboard that supported the candlesticks—all as ordinary as sin.

There was a painting above the mantel of a tragical woman in an old-fashioned blue dress. Most likely the old man's mother—else why was she there? And what could be more ordinary than that? No: there was nothing uncanny anywhere.

'Now, young man—your name, *if* you please?'

'Partridge. Benjamin Partridge.'

'And . . . and the *other* name?'

'Corbett. Apothecary Corbett of Gospel Oak.'

The old man wrote carefully, then sanded the paper and put it away in a drawer. While he was engaged, Benjamin peered round the room once more.

The wall facing the window was taken up with shelves. Shelves from floor to ceiling. Shelves about a foot apart and divided into pigeon-holes.

So the old man liked pigeon-holes? Nothing chilling in that. What did he keep in them? Impossible to see. Sharp shadows obscured each opening—save one. A gleam of white could be seen. Benjamin stared.

Lord! Was it—was it a *pudding bowl*? Yes indeed! And cracked. Benjamin all but grinned at the absurdity of it.

'Have you,' said the old man gently, 'anything about you that *he* has touched lately? Anything will do. Just so long as he's touched it and his warmth's been upon it.'

Benjamin started. The old man had left the desk and was standing before him, hand outstretched. Confusedly, he felt in his pockets and found the empty jar for the 'piece of a ghost'.

'Yes!' said the boy angrily. 'Here's something he touched! Rot him!'

'All in good time,' said the old man, and took the jar.

He examined it carefully . . . so carefully that his withered old lips seemed to touch it.

What now? He began to fish about in his pockets. (Lord, he must have been wearing as many coats as a hackney carriage driver!)

At last he found what he wanted. Nothing worse than a length of black ribbon.

Without another glance at the boy, he wound it round the neck of the jar and tied it in a curious knot. Then he took up a candle and shuffled over to the wall of shelves. As he drew near, he raised the candle so that by chance it illumined each and every pigeon-hole.

Now the boy's soul grew cold as ice. He shook and he shuddered. A chill crept through his veins.

In each of the pigeon-holes lay a singular item. An item of no great value. An item that bore no relation to its neighbour—save in one thing.

Here, there was a pincushion; there, a pair of spectacles; beneath, was a silver fork; beside it, a lace handkerchief—and beside that, a child's doll, very fixed-looking. In one hole, there lay a pistol, and in another, a piece of wax candle . . .

Items as far apart as could be imagined, with but one odd, trifling thing in common. Each had tied about it, and fastened with a curious knot, a piece of black ribbon!

'It's done,' said the old man quietly. Mister Corbett's jar had joined its neighbours.

'Is he . . . he is . . . dead now?' whispered Benjamin, unable to tear his eyes from that wall of mortal hate.

'In minutes, young man. Nothing can save him now. No need to worry. If you leave directly, you'll see it. Come, young man—it's nearly time.'

But, try as he might, Benjamin could not look away from the shelved wall. He'd seen a hat he thought he knew. The hat of a gentleman who had lived nearby— till he'd died last month: much beloved, universally mourned.

Who had brought that hat?

The old man sensed the boy's distress. He moved the candle away from the wall so that all the pigeon-holes sank back into their separate blacknesses.

'Everyone fancies they recognize an item there,' he murmured. 'But, believe me, it's most unlikely. It really is!'

He took the boy's arm. 'Now you must hurry. Back to the road, else you'll miss him. And that would never do! After all, it's the chief part of what you're paying for!'

His fingers were strong. They fumbled down to the boy's bone causing sharp pains to inhabit his arm from shoulder to finger-tips.

There were no more words between them. The old man snuffed the unnecessary candle and, holding the other, drew Benjamin from the room.

Where was the black ribboned jar? On which shelf? Vainly, the boy glared over his shoulder as he was pulled from the room. All was darkness: his own offering not to be distinguished among dolls, spectacles, and pudding bowls. Such an insignificant thing was his hatred!

Silently—save for the sound of his own rough breathing and the old man's snuffles—they went down the stairs and back to the front door.

Not so much as a: Good night, young man, did the old man utter; still less a: Happy New Year. Maybe he thought he'd already done enough in that direction?

All he said as they stood momentarily on the porch was: 'Remember, Benjamin Partridge of Gospel Oak, a quarter of your life's earnings. Monthly. My usual terms.

Now, hurry or you'll miss it! His time's all but at full stretch!'

Did he then push the boy back on to the path? Or did Benjamin stumble? He fell face down and heard the door shut and the knocker tremble faintly.

He got to his feet. His fall, and now the general night damp, conspired to make him vilely cold. He pushed his hands into his pockets and found the old man's medicine—still undelivered.

He turned to go back. The porch light was doused. The house—more like a great undertaker than ever—was of a misty black. He shivered, and turned again towards the high road.

He'd been advised to hurry. So hurry he did: along the disquieting path that sobbed under his feet like a heart-broken child . . .

At last he reached the road. Thank God, the wind was much diminished. Overhead the clouds hung in vague, disturbing shapes—some horned, some winged, some with jaws agape.

There came a sound of running feet. He looked along the road towards Highgate. His heart quickened. He began to sweat.

Towards him, limping and panting, spectacles agleam in the moon (whose light did nothing but bad for his leprous complexion), came Mister Corbett!

Nearer and nearer he came. Was he grinning? How ugly were his teeth!

But what now? His bony hands reached out—as if he would clutch and speak. To say what? Nothing.

Even as he reached to touch the boy his face curdled, his eyes fell up, and his mouth fell down in a long, black O.

The old man had done his business capably. Mister Corbett was dead. His body dropped down in the road. And over it stood Benjamin Partridge: revenged.

There was not much of pleasure on the boy's face. He was not situated for it. Alone he stood, under the high night, beside the corpse of the master he'd wished dead with all his heart and soul.

'I didn't do it,' he whispered uneasily. 'I never touched him!'

CHAPTER FOUR

'You asked for it, Mister Corbett! As the moon's my witness, you asked for it! One kind word out of you and I'd not have gone to the house. As this moon above is my witness!'

Benjamin Partridge turned from the corpse and peered at the moon: his witness.

His witness! Fearfully he stared up and along the road. Who else, beside the moon, had seen? No one. Not a living soul anywhere—save his own.

With difficulty, he smiled . . . then caught Mister Corbett's eye. Disagreeably, the apothecary's spectacles still shone in the moonlight. Being lifeless, they'd failed to die.

'I'm off now, Mister Corbett. And there's nothing you can say that'll keep me this time!'

He began to walk, but soon stopped and looked back. There lay the corpse, face upward, silently shouting to the moon.

Benjamin swallowed, but there was no moisture in his throat. He attempted to walk again. A frightening thought struck him. What if he should meet with someone while the dead apothecary was still in sight? Would not that someone put two and two together and make an unfavourable four?

'Murderer!' they'd shout 'Murderer! He's murdered his master! Catch him! Hang him!'

No doubt about it. With much circumspection he began to creep back.

Dear God! How them spectacles shone under the moon! Fair blazed, they did! Once more, he stood by the dead man. Best move him off the road. Best tumble him among the bushes. Blame the footpads. Blame the weather, even—but don't blame Benjamin! *He* never laid a finger on him.

Damn the old man! Why did he have to fetch Mister Corbett out on to the road to give up his dingy ghost? Why couldn't the perishing have been quiet and respectable in bed? Or even in the shop? Just dropped down behind the counter like an old broom?

'Rot you, Mister Corbett! You're as horrible dead as alive! But not for long!'

He bent down and seized hold of the apothecary's coat and pulled with all his might.

'You're a dead weight, Mister Corbett, skinny that you are! Your bones must be made of . . . of lead!'

The apothecary's head dropped down on to his chest, as if apologizing for the trouble he was giving his apprentice.

They were at the edge of the road. One more heave and Mister Corbett would be safely over it and rolling down into the spotted dark.

How queer the gleaming patches looked, for the phosphorescence caught off the earlier rain still persisted. Maybe it was even more remarkable than before: like a fine fall of stars.

No. More like eyes. Why, they seemed to be in pairs!

'One last heave and it's goodbye for ever, Mister Corbett!'

Benjamin made ready. Glanced once more along the road. Peace and quiet either way.

'Sleep well, Mister—'

The spots of light! They were shifting. Impossible! The circumstance was distracting him—unsettling his sight. And small wonder!

'Sleep well, Mist—'

They *were* moving! They were circling about. They were creeping nearer and nearer, and always in pairs. They *were* eyes!

The boy let go of his burden with a cry of dismay. The Heath was alive! Dark and obscure shapes were rising up from it. Shapes of ragged, powerful men. A dozen, fifteen—even twenty of them. Monstrous fellows who stared and grinned and scowled.

'Coming with us, young 'un?' murmured a voice. 'For it looks like that's where you belongs!'

'Done 'im in,' muttered another admiringly. 'Neat as kiss-your-'and. Needle, knife, or skewer, young 'un? What did you use? My, but you're a nifty slicer!'

'I . . . I never touched him,' whispered Benjamin, half out of his mind with terror.

'We all know that one!' mumbled a third voice, fruity with phlegm. 'We've all tried that one—from time to time. "Never touched 'im, yer Honour. 'E just fell dead at me feet!" But they 'angs you just the same, young 'un.'

On which there was a confused sound of agreement and these violent, desolate creatures from the darkness began to climb up and over the edge of the road.

Very bushy they were about the chops, and thorny and horny in their skins. They were the lurking murderers and footpads of the Heath.

'Neat . . . very neat indeed,' mumbled a foxy brute with a torn cheek. 'Get you five shilling a time for work like that anywheres. What say, young 'un? Make a tidy forchun between us. Never seed a man dropped so neat!'

'I never touched him,' moaned Benjamin: on which the felons laughed silently, exposing their broken teeth to the moon.

'You'd best come along with us, young 'un,' repeated the first speaker. He was a tall, lean man with some rags of authority about him. Maybe a dismissed sergeant or the mate of some doubtful ship?

He made to lay his hand on Benjamin's shoulder, but the boy shrank back. The man stank to the stars.

'Not good enough for you, you little grey-faced rat? Giving yourself airs? You'll be sorry for that!'

Angrily he turned to his companions. 'Don't no one 'elp 'im. Though 'is back may break and 'is 'eart may crack, don't no one 'elp 'im. We ain't good enough for 'im. So let's be going, brothers.'

Now there followed a truly dismal sight. One by one, each of these grim men turned to the dark of the Heath and one by one came back, bearing a heavy burden. Drunken wayfarers, boozed horseboys who'd missed their way, servants who'd taken short cuts, even a youth who'd strayed to look for his hat the wind had blown away. Old men, young men, men who'd been in the prime of their lives, now lying like dull old bags across powerful shoulders—in the prime of their deaths. Murdered, each and every one.

But none so neatly as Mister Corbett.

'Makes you ashamed, don't it?' wheezed the foxy man, who grunted under a fat coachman he'd drowned in the Whitestone Pond.

'W-where are you going?' whispered Benjamin, whose terror, by this time, had passed all mortal bounds.

'To the Highgate graveyards,' replied the foxy one softly, as if anxious not to be heard talking to him. 'We always does. Can't leave our 'andiwork to rot and betray us, can we? We buries it, friend—good and deep.'

They were all upon the road again. The tall man, who wore his corpse like a bulky halter, nodded, and the melancholy procession began to shuffle along the road to Highgate.

'Best come along, young 'un—else you'll be took and 'anged.'

'But I never touched him!' moaned Benjamin piteously. 'They can't hang me for nothing!'

But who would believe him? In all truth, his situation was not promising. The abominable Mister Corbett gaped accusingly up at him. Plainly his chief hope lay with those who, from experience, knew best.

He bent down and seized Mister Corbett's chilly wrists. He pulled and heaved and strained. His back cracked, his heart nearly burst, but at last Mister Corbett was folded across his shoulder with a bony hip digging into Benjamin's neck.

It was monstrously uncomfortable, but none the less, with tottering steps he hastened on, striving to overtake the glum crew ahead.

Which was not difficult, for his horrible foxy friend with the fat, wet coachman loitered and complained of his lot.

'Catch me death,' he kept muttering. ' 'E's soaking through to me lungs. 'E must 'ave took up 'alf the pond inside of 'im. For that's what 'e's discharging now! Still— I saved 'is watch from a wetting, so it weren't for nothing. It's an ill wind, as they say! What did you prig from your'n, young 'un?'

Benjamin, who'd thieved nothing from Mister Corbett save his life, felt suddenly awkward and almost ashamed.

'How much farther?' he panted. 'He's growing that heavy!'

'Leastways, he ain't wet,' mumbled the drowner. 'Leastways, you'll not be catching your death! Be thankful you got a skill, young 'un, and can drop 'em neat. Make a forchun between us—if you should change your mind!'

Benjamin shook his head as best he could against the obstruction of the dead apothecary and shuddered. Not for the hugest fortune in the world would he have joined this dreadful procession nightly. All he longed for was to get Mister Corbett safely underground.

There was a halt ahead. Much shuffling and grunting

and soft cursing as dead arms gently swung and smacked the backs that had borne them. Why the delay? Constables? God forbid! No: they were arrived at the toll-house.

Formidable legality: not to be avoided.

A copper oil lamp hung on a bracket outside the toll-house, lighting the list of tolls.

For a man and a horse . . . one penny halfpenny.
For a man, a horse and cart . . . fourpence halfpenny.
For a coach and four horses . . . one shilling and sixpence.
For cattle, sheep, pigs . . . two shillings the score or part thereof.
For a man and a corpse . . . seven shillings and sixpence.

Lord, but the turnpike keeper took a mean advantage! But in the circumstances, what could a poor murderer do? Pay up—or be hanged!

'Pay up or be hanged!' joked the keeper as the grim gentry crowded at the gate.

'Rogue!' 'Villain!' 'Lousy thief!' 'Stinking robber!' were the various greetings, spoke low and weary.

There came a general heaving as of a black mountainous sea, followed by the clink of coin as hands went to obstructed pockets and found the passage money.

One by one they payed up and passed on, till at last it was Benjamin's turn.

'Pay up or be hanged!' grinned the keeper, hand out-stretched.

'Four shillings. That's all I've got,' mumbled Benjamin.

'Don't no one 'elp 'im!' called out the lean man sourly.

'Sorry, young 'un,' breathed the foxy gent. 'Can't afford new friends in our line of business. See you in hell, maybe.'

With that he turned his back and shuffled off into the dark towards the Highgate graveyards, with the drowned coachman weeping over his shoulder and seeming to wave a shrewd goodbye.

Very soon, they were gone—the creeping murderers—
and even the creaking of their feet was lost in the ordinary
sounds of the night . . .

'Pay up—or be hanged,' repeated the keeper.

'For God's sake, sir, won't you take my four shillings?
I got to get through! Can't you see, I got to bury him?'

The keeper shook his crafty head.

'Sorry, lad. No exceptions, else where would we be?
Letting 'em all through for sixpence in no time!'

'Then . . . then I'll leave him and be gone alone!' cried
Benjamin in violent desperation.

'Oh, no you don't, lad! I want none of *your* rubbish left
here! Be off with you—*and* take your quiet friend! Lord,
but he's an ugly customer all right.'

'But I can't run no farther! My back's breaking and
my heart's on the burst! Take pity on me!'

'Sorry, lad. There's no room for pity in our line of
business. You must take your chances with your ugly
friend; and I fancy they ain't so good.' He cocked his head
on a far-off sound. 'Don't want to depress you, lad, but
there's a coach on its way. And coming quick. Yes, lad,
I'm a-fancying your time's come. And all for the want of
another three and sixpence.'

'But I never touched him! I never touched him!'

On which the keeper laughed, then laughed louder
yet, for the lumbered apprentice had begun to run . . .

Dear God in heaven, what a piece of running it was.
All the devils in hell must have screamed with merriment
at it! This way—that way—tottering, capering, panting
his lungs up in a manner most pitiful, while the dead
apothecary kept thumping his back with stiff arms like he
was no better than a beast of burden.

He staggered to the side of the road, for the coach was
coming. Already he could see it, dark and implacable,
with the cold moon gleaming on its carved edges.

He groaned and knelt as if in prayer.

'May you rest in peace, Mister Corbett: and give *me* peace at last! Goodbye to you—for ever!

With a roar and a clatter the coach came racketing close. The horses plunged and shrieked. The huddled coachman shouted: dragged at the reins.

'Madman! Madman!'

A man—the figure of a man—had toppled drunkenly into the road: seemed almost to have been pushed. The coach halted. A white-faced boy came running.

'He's dead! I saw it! He fell in your way! Run down! The coach killed him! I saw it!'

Benjamin Partridge, rid at last of his burden, came panting to the door of the coach.

'An accident!' he cried excitedly. 'No one to blame! I saw it all!'

The coach door opened. Darkness within. Came a cold voice, attended by a snuffle: 'Did you indeed, Benjamin Partridge?'

It was the old man!

CHAPTER FIVE

'Why do you tremble and shudder, Benjamin Partridge? Why do you groan as if in anguish? Why is your face as deathly as the moon?'

The old man spoke softly, but Benjamin was not deceived: softness was not in *his* line of business.

'Why are you suddenly silent, Benjamin Partridge?' pursued the old man. 'And why do you spread out your arms as if to hide your dead friend? It *is* Mister Corbett, ain't it?'

He peered sideways at the crumpled corpse that lay behind the boy, its spectacles all awry and shining brokenly.

'Why do you cover your face with your hands and shake as if your soul has taken the ague? Come, young man, answer me.'

'Help me—help me!' whispered Benjamin. 'I can't get through the gate. I can't bury him. Help me—or I'll be hanged!'

'Very likely, young man. Very likely you will be.'

'But—' began Benjamin, then stopped. To plead once more he'd never touched his dead master would not be taken amiably by the old man. There'd be a difference of opinion. Benjamin saw it in his sharp, bright eyes.

The old man seemed in no hurry to be gone, even though his coachman shifted impatiently in the cold night air. Once or twice, Benjamin caught his reproachful glance ('Tried to blame me, did you?'), but his face was so shadowed, it was hard to be sure . . .

'But if I'm hanged, I'll not be able to pay you!' cried Benjamin suddenly. (Surely the old man would protect a customer?)

'True enough, young man. And it wouldn't be the first
time. You'd be amazed,' he went on, shaking his head as
if *he* was amazed, 'how often gentlemen don't pay me. If
it's on account of judge and jury, I don't quarrel with it.
No one's to blame there. But there's a surprising number
who do wild things to avoid payment. Yes, indeed. Hang
themselves, shoot themselves, drown themselves, poison
themselves, even dash out their brains against the walls of
Bedlam! The world's very full of men who fancy it to be
more honourable to die than to pay their debts.'

He paused and sighed.

'But you're not one of them, Benjamin Partridge, are
you? You've an honest face—even though it's white as
bone!'

'No,' muttered Benjamin, sinking into a pit of despair
so deep that the moon seemed more than ordinarily
remote. 'I'm not one of them.'

Drearily he stared down at the dead apothecary whose
weight was dragging him to the gallows.

'He's only mutton, so to speak,' murmured the old
man. 'He can't harm you now. Though his eyes seem to
stare, they don't really. He cannot haunt you, young man.
It's not as though he was a ghost.'

'If only he was!' cried Benjamin. 'It's his dead weight
that's killing me! I can't go on. My heart's on the burst.
Oh, if only he was a ghost!'

'Heart and soul,' the old man reminded him. 'And
now the heart proves too weak. What of the soul,
Benjamin Partridge? Could your soul carry a ghost? Or
would that prove too weak likewise? Consider, young
man. Think carefully. Even supposing it was possible,
might not a ghost prove too heavy for your soul?'

'*Is* it—is it possible?' whispered Benjamin, spying a
faint hope that the old man was melted by pity. A light,
easy, effortless phantom would be a wonderful exchange
for the terrible corpse.

'All things are possible to the willing soul.'

'Then . . . will you—?'

The old man was overtaken by a fit of sniffling and snuffling that lasted out the passage of a cloud across the moon. Darkness shadowed him till he spoke again.

'I bear you no ill will, young man: not even for trying to lay your victim at my coach door. In my line of business that's common. All I ask is that your soul should be willing.'

'Yes—yes—yes! It is.'

The old man shrugged his shoulders.

'Fetch down my box,' he said to the coachman; and that surly, humped and shadowy figure grunted with displeasure, for the box was large and awkward and cost great efforts to get down.

At last, with a faint jarring, it was set in the road, stout enough and tall enough for the old man to step down upon as he came out of the coach.

With mounting hope, Benjamin watched. To tell the truth, his present circumstance was such that any change would be of a hopeful nature.

The old man fished in his many coats for the key, while the coachman swung his arms vigorously and stamped his feet to keep warm.

The key was found and the old man knelt and unlocked the box. The coachman shivered and swung his arms more vigorously than ever, as if a deeper chill was come into the air.

'I take them wherever I go,' said the old man, lifting the lid and displaying the telltale items from his wall of shelves. 'For they're my only livelihood. My house has been broke into this many a night by . . . by gentlemen. Can you imagine it? Ah! Right on top! How fortunate we are!'

He lifted out Mister Corbett's jar and peered at it in the light of the moon. Abruptly, he stood upright and turned to Benjamin. The road must have sloped thereabouts, and the old man been on an eminence, for he now seemed taller than Benjamin—by an inch or more.

'Hold it for me,' he said, and Benjamin took the jar with trembling hands.

'Some folks tie lovers' knots,' he murmured, more to himself than to Benjamin. 'But we tie haters' knots, don't we, young man? Now—now—now it's done!'

He took back the jar with its black ribbon, in which there was now a second knot.

'Look, Benjamin Partridge! Behold your ghost!'

CHAPTER SIX

Before Benjamin's eyes—his amazed eyes—the apothecary's corpse was on the turn. It had begun to quake and seethe like milk neglected on the hob. Its thin hands seemed to overflow till, where there had been ten fingers, there were now twenty. Likewise the stockinged legs, the old brown breeches, the waistcoat with its stains of oil of camphor and smears of sulphur, the coat (his best), the woollen scarf that he, Benjamin, had given him on his first Christmas—and ever after prayed would choke him—all most subtly and silently boiled over till there was a second Mister Corbett rising like steam unequally from the first.

Extraordinary sight. But not yet done with. Consider the solid Mister Corbett, lying limp and disagreeable under the charitable moon. Being empty, his sides sank in, his face diminished, and the whole of him shuddered into a flabby nothingness—like a shrunken balloon. Then this, too, shrank and came down to a tiny spot of damp that might have been dew.

'No more to him than that?' whispered Benjamin wonderingly to the old man. There was no answer. Benjamin turned. The road was quiet; the coach had gone. So absorbed had he been in the emptying of Mister Corbett, that all sound must have escaped him. Once more he was alone with the perished apothecary.

But the difference—oh, the difference! Beside him now, with both feet almost on the ground, stood the apothecary's ghost.

Gone was the gloomy weight, the listless, damning sack of flesh and bone and halted blood. In its place was a Mister Corbett better than new. Not the sharpest eye could have told he was not what he seemed. This fellow could be passed off anywhere as the genuine apothecary.

Down to the same blueness about the chin and the same mole on the side of his nose, it was Mister Corbett. Even Benjamin, though he'd seen every inch rise up uncannily, was momentarily deceived.

'Mister Corbett, sir—' he said uneasily.

But the ghost did not reply. It stood and stared at the boy in a manner most timidly solemn, like a child on its first day in school.

Now triumph, joy, and amazement struggled in Benjamin's breast. His misery was at an end. He felt—yes, he felt in that moment almost pleased to see the luckless man looking so much like himself.

'Mister Corbett!' he cried, and took a pace forward.

The ghost shrank back.

'Mister Corbett!' repeated Benjamin, advancing another step.

The ghost shuddered and put up its imitation arms as if to defend itself.

'Mister Corbett,' said Benjamin for a third time, with much of the triumph gone from his voice. The ghost's aspect was not encouraging to it: its face expressed terror.

A cold discomfort entered the boy. He thrust his hands into his pockets with an air of defiance.

'What are you staring at, Mister Corbett?'

The terror in the phantom's eyes grew extreme. Mister Corbett was staring at the apprentice who had hated him.

'I . . . I never touched you, you know,' said Benjamin, and wondered if Mister Corbett had any notion of what had befallen him: if he knew of the house and the black ribbon and the desolate murderers' walk.

Being a spirit, no doubt such knowledge was possible to it. Benjamin shivered. Was it likewise possible that it knew now—for the first time—the scope of the apprentice's hate?

'You brought it on yourself, Mister Corbett. You were as hard as iron,' said Benjamin unhappily.

The ghost's lips moved. Benjamin strained to hear. The voice was all but withered away, having no solid organ at its origin to give it resonance and substance.

'I—am—in—hell . . .'

'No you ain't!' cried Benjamin indignantly, for he was frightened beyond measure at such a striking notion. 'You're on Hampstead Heath, Mister Corbett, as well you must know!'

But the news did not seem to cheer the apothecary's ghost tremendously, and its dread of its murderer did not seem much abated.

'Cold. I am so cold,' it moaned, and plucked at its scarf in that mean and finicky way Mister Corbett had so often plucked at it when he'd been alive.

'It's a cold night, Mister Corbett, so there's nothing unnatural in your feeling it. If—'

He stopped. There was someone coming. A horseman. He whipped round the bend in the road too quick for Benjamin to hide.

'Happy New Year to the pair of you!' shouted the rider, and galloped on.

Benjamin wiped the sweat from his brow.

'The Lord be praised, Mister Corbett! He took you for a living man!'

Sadly, the phantom nodded.

'A living man, Mister Corbett! Think of it! It's only me that knows you're not!'

Filled now with a fine, nervous determination to make the best of his situation, he began to walk back towards the turnpike.

Then a grim thought struck him. What if the ghost should seek revenge? What if it should accuse him? Was that not the proper office of ghosts?

Several times he turned, longing desperately to ask,

'Would you betray me, Mister Corbett?' But each time
the question stuck in his throat and the ghost came on,
bent-shouldered, stooping, with that aggravating spying
air he'd ever had in life.

'I'm so cold!' it moaned. 'So very cold!' And it continued
to spy and peer as if for a warm corner somewhere.

'So it's you again, lad!' said the turnpike keeper, hanging
his head out of his window like a battered sign. Then he
saw the apothecary's ghost. He stared.

'I thought—' he began. 'I could have sworn—' he
began again. 'I could have taken my oath that—'

'It turned out that he was only poorly,' said Benjamin,
his heart beating furiously. 'And now he's as good as
new.'

'I'd have gone bail for his being dead as mutton!'
muttered the keeper, shaking his head, while the ghost of
Mister Corbett returned his stare in a chilly, melancholy
fashion, but spoke not a word.

'Poorly, you said? Now you come to mention it, he
does look a bit pale around the chops. And, no offence, it
don't improve him any.'

'I'm so cold!' whispered the ghost at last.

'Cold, is he? Not surprised. He ain't dressed over warm.
If you've any Christian charity in you, lad (as I hopes is in
every mortal soul!) take him into the Spaniards' Inn for a tot
of brandy and rum. Half and half, with a sprig of rosemary.
That'll put roses in his cheeks! Go on, lad! Be a Christian on
this New Year's Eve and warm your freezing friend!'

With all his heart the boy longed to go into the inn,
for it was a cheerful place. Its windows shone and there
was a smell of roast and onions in the air. But he feared
the ghost's accusing finger . . . and cry of 'Murderer!'

'Go on, lad!' urged the keeper, a powerful minder of
the world's business.

'Directly! Directly!' cried Benjamin, backing towards

the inn and wondering how best he could escape. God knew whether the warmth of a parlour might not give the ghost strength for his damaging cry!

'Would you betray me?' he whispered desperately.

'Betray you?' echoed the apothecary's ghost.

'Accuse me for . . . for revenge—?'

'What would I want with revenge? I am in hell and want for—'

But what the phantom wanted for was drowned out by the keeper's impatient cries of 'Hurry, there!' for his kindliness was of an interfering, bullying sort.

'Directly! Directly!' answered Benjamin.

'D'you want help with your friend?'

'No! No!'

He took the spectre's hand. An unpleasant moment, that. Not so much the chill (as of a piece of cold air), but the lack of substance. There was nothing to grasp. His fingers closed in on themselves. Horrible.

He glanced back to see if the keeper had noticed. But for once that nosy fellow had seen nothing.

'A near thing, Mister Corbett,' breathed Benjamin. 'We must be careful. Though you *look* as good as new, there's less to you than meets the eye.'

They had entered the inn yard where tall coaches stood upon the moon-washed cobbles like dark ships becalmed on a silver sea.

Once more Benjamin stopped. The inn beckoned— but he was afraid. He stared back. The keeper was watching them all the way.

'Give you a hand?' he bellowed.

God forbid! Benjamin shook his head and hurried on. Abruptly, a horseboy scuttled from the stables back to the warmth of the inn. He saw the wayfarers—even crossed their path—and briefly waved. He never noticed the uncanny circumstance of two figures approaching with but the sound of a single pair of feet.

This gave Benjamin a touch of confidence, but not very much of it. He glanced sideways at his murdered master, shuffling stoop-shouldered as though his overlong scarf was weighing him down.

He's bound to betray me, thought Benjamin gloomily, no matter what he says. It's in his nature to betray me.

But the ghost only shuddered and moaned: 'I'm so cold. Who would have thought hell to be so cold?'

Benjamin Partridge bit his lip till the blood came.

'You're no more in hell than I am, Mister Corbett. And well you must know it! It's a cold night—'

'What's keeping you now, lad?' came the keeper's voice, surly with charitable intent.

A lamp swung gently in the inn's porch. To mark the New Year and good resolutions, someone had polished it and the landlord had bought clean oil. It burned brightly and set off the timber work to advantage.

Benjamin sighed. Sooner or later there was a world to be mingled with. Was not here and now as good a place and time as any?

'You'll not betray me, Mister Corbett? You swear you'll not betray me?'

The ghost looked at him in terror and grief.

'Not I! Not I!'

'All right, Mister Corbett. We'll go into the warm, then.'

They passed under the porch lamp. As they did so, Benjamin's confidence suffered a sharp decline. He had made a detestable discovery. He had seen the lamp through the phantom's head! In the light—in a good light—the apothecary's ghost was transparent!

CHAPTER SEVEN

O nce within the inn, a thousand fears had invaded him. Every flicker of flame had terrified him; every sudden leap of the fire, every glow of a lighted pipe had given him such dread as only the deepest shadows could partly dispel.

'For pity's sake, Mister Corbett—keep out of the light!'

Desolately the phantom had returned his frantic looks, as if unaware of its own infirmity. It hung its head, ashamed of it knew not what . . . and followed its murderer close by the darkest wall of the candlelit parlour.

It was now half after eleven and the parlour was filled with travellers and their servants, briefly united in the fellowship of the hour. The New Year drew nigh and, as the wine flowed down, good resolutions flowed out, tempered with a rosy whiff of claret.

'Merciful heaven, Mister Corbett! Draw in your shoulder! Oh God! I can see that gentleman's face as plain as day through you!'

The phantom exposed its ugly teeth in a semblance of Mister Corbett's unpleasant smile . . . and drew back against the wall with a pitiful air of shame.

'Thank you, Mister Corbett. That was uncommon obliging of you!'

A dozen times already, he'd had occasion to thank Mister Corbett with such urgent gratitude. Not that the phantom had put itself in the way of discovery, but there were a terrible number of tapers and candles going about the parlour like fireflies, to light extinguished pipes, read letters, admire trifles of lace, even to search for a dropped half-penny.

And each time, Benjamin's heart chilled as he glimpsed the flame through the phantom's substance. It seemed not possible that such an eerie thing had passed unnoticed. Yet neighbours in the room—good, respectable folk—continued to smile at him and murdered Mister Corbett and raise their tankards politely whenever their eyes turned that way. He believed he'd collected enough 'Happy New Years' to see him out at a hundred; and each one provoked more anguish than the last.

With all manner of twistings and turnings and leanings forward, he struggled to cast Mister Corbett into the shadows. An evil moment came when a pair of tankards were passed along the line, one for him and one for the pallid gentleman by his side—'with the compliments of the House'.

Frantic was his reaching to keep a hold on the second tankard: yet with deep caution lest he poke his arm, hand, tankard and all clean through Mister Corbett. And all the while, that murdered man sat silent by his side, with never a look nor a sound that was not obligingly lifelike; never a reproach on his murderer save in the deathly chill that came from his person and chilled Benjamin's shoulder, arm, and thigh.

But what was he doing now, that cold, cold ghost? In fear and anger, Benjamin suddenly became aware of the phantom's singular behaviour.

First a hand, then a foot, then a hand again it was slyly holding up before the fire. It was charmed by its own transparency! On its face was that self-same look that Benjamin had known so well in life—a deep, absorbed and searching look . . .

'Good God, Mister Corbett! What are you at? You will betray us!'

Guiltily the ghost snatched back its hand and shrank once more into the shade. Piteous were its eyes as it peered at Benjamin, and its thin lips moved unhappily: 'I'll not betray . . . only, give me warmth . . . forgive—'

Gloomily, Benjamin nodded. Unthinking and even childish as the ghost's action had been, he was, after all, lately only human.

Strangeness must still have interested him; company still pleased him; a fire still warmed him. And though he still had Mister Corbett's ugly smile, and Mister Corbett's spying stoop, and Mister Corbett's mean and furtive air, there was a sharp sadness in it all.

'You are a poor soul,' whispered Benjamin impulsively, but the ghost shuddered as if in profound dismay.

'I'll not betray . . . not I!'

'That's uncommon obliging of you, Mister Corbett, sir . . . and I believe you with all my heart.'

Suddenly there was a cry of 'Make way! Make way!' and two servants attended by the landlord and his lady came grandly in with a silver bowl of punch. The room was filled with the hot sweet odours of brandy, spice, and the Lord knew what else besides. The Spaniards' punch was a deep secret, and, though many a man had been told it, the cunning spirit fuddled him too much to remember its recipe and carry it home on New Year's Day in the morning.

At once there was a general shifting towards the table in the middle of the parlour—and consequently some space was left before the fire.

The fire. Benjamin saw the phantom stare at it with longing. What with the cheerfulness of the parlour following so hard on his late adventure, and the general obligingness of the ghost, he was moved more deeply than he'd bargained for. He discovered he was not so inhuman as to hate Mister Corbett beyond the grave.

'I'll go stand before the fire, Mister Corbett,' he whispered, 'and then you may stand behind me and warm yourself. No one will see while they're at the punch bowl. Come, sir, move as I move . . . exactly . . . but for mercy's sake, be careful!'

With extraordinary caution, Benjamin stood up and

stepped sideways before the fire. He might have been a single figure, though a trifle rheumaticky, for his movements appeared peculiarly stiff and slow.

At last, distinctly—most distinctly—Benjamin heard the phantom sigh and sensed that it rubbed its hands together in Mister Corbett's old oily fashion.

'Are you warm now, Mister Corbett?'

'The fire burns bright,' came the faint reply, and Benjamin smiled benevolently.

In the middle of the room punch was being ladled out in a capacious silver spoon, 'with the compliments of the House'. Much was the noise and entertainment there, and no one spared a glance towards the fire.

'At last, Mister Corbett—a real piece of luck!'

'I make it five minutes more!' suddenly declared a gentleman, consulting his watch.

'Eight,' corrected the landlord. 'It's eight minutes in this house, sir.'

Then someone else—most probably the landlord's lady herself, a respectable, kindly woman—discovered it to be three minutes only to the New Year.

Directly, there was an amiable commotion. Why? Nothing alarming, nothing dreadful—or even disquieting. So why did Benjamin Partridge turn white and glare horribly about him?

'Hands, gents! Hands must be joined!' shouted the landlord, and stretched out his portly arms like a well-fed signpost.

'Come, sirs!' cried his lady above the hubbub, and took one of her husband's hands, 'A circle, now! All join hands for the New Year! You, sir—and you—and you over there! No one must be left out! They say it's bad luck—'

Remorselessly the happy, laughing chain grew as more and more hands were joined. Nearer and nearer the fire it came.

Hands twisting, clutching, grasping, madly dancing,

seemed everywhere. Frantically Benjamin stared to his right. A hand as gnarled as a gibbet reached out to complete its chain. He turned to the left. A hand with veins like a hangman's rope reached likewise.

'Got you, young man!' shouted a voice in his ear. His right hand was seized!

'The last link! The last link!' came the cry—for Benjamin had been jerked aside to make way for the last link. Who was it? Why, that pale fellow behind.

'Last link! Last—'

Before the flaming fire, the last link stood pitilessly revealed. A weak link indeed!

Stoop-shouldered, grinning dingily like the Death's Head it was, stood the apothecary's ghost. And the fire was seen burning—right through him!

Hands felt hands tremble and sweat, then grip hard as iron . . . then withdraw from each other. Faces grew pale. In the midst of goodwill, in the midst of hope and merriment, what had stalked in?

All began to draw away, shaking with horror at the sight of the phantom: all save the boy who had brought it in. Wretchedly and shamefully, he stood beside murdered Mister Corbett.

'Not I! Not I!' whispered the ghost.

'Murderer!' cried someone harshly and pointed to Benjamin Partridge.

'It was him who brought the ghost! Murderer!'

The cry was taken up in every corner of the room. Even the cheerful, spotty potboy by the punch bowl screamed, 'Murderer!' with his face screwed up in anger, fear, and disgust.

'Be gone before the New Year strikes! Get out and take your damnation with you!'

'Outcast! Wicked, hateful outcast! How dared you come among us?'

'Break the glass he drank from!'

'Scour the seat he sat on!'

'Let out the air he breathed!'

'Open the window! Open the door! For he's—'

In the misery of his shame, Benjamin Partridge put his hands to his ears and rushed for the open door. Close on his heels followed the apothecary's ghost, whose chill and despairing aspect repelled all pursuit.

'Not I! Not I!' it moaned. '*I* did not betray!'

CHAPTER EIGHT

The clouds were gone and the moon and the stars inherited the black sky. Despairingly the boy and the phantom passed along the whited high road: two figures with but a single shadow.

Where were they going? What home would take them in? Which family would not turn pale with dread and disgust?

The boy walked rapidly; the ghost shuffled desolately in his wake. The distance between them never exceeded a yard, hasten as the boy might. Was it possible he was trying to out-distance the ghost? Maybe . . . but his soul was too darkened by the loss of all his hopes to know distinctly where he was going, or why.

He paused. An iron sound filled the air. The bells of St Michael-on-the-Hill were tolling the hour. Midnight. In the distance other bells likewise beat and swung and chimed. The very night seemed a house of bells; and faintly, in between the chimes, came a sound of laughter, cheering, and delight. Secure in their parlours, warm and gleaming families rejoiced.

'A happy New Year to you, Mister Corbett,' wept Benjamin, thinking of where those words might have been spoken: in whose company—and by whose fire.

'I did not betray you!' moaned the ghost—to whom all years were, henceforth, alike, and none of them happy. 'Not I.'

'I betrayed *you* —'

'Willingly? Was it *willingly* done?'

Once more those hated words—but, oh, the painful difference! Such a world of pleading and piteous eagerness was there in '*willingly*', that Benjamin could not but nod and reassure the unhappy ghost.

'You were so cold—'

'Hell is cold . . .'

'You were in the Spaniards', sir—on my honour you were!'

But the ghost whispered softly, 'No tavern, tomb, inn or rest for the murdered man. Only a place in his murderer's cold mansion of hate.'

Benjamin shook his head.

'I don't hate you any more, Mister Corbett. I've had my fill of revenge.'

'So where must we go, you and I? Everywhere, I must go with you.'

The boy looked about him at the wild and lonely Heath. Darker still grew his spirit. The prospect before him was dismal in the extreme.

'The woods . . . the fields . . . the dark corners . . . forsaken places . . . the bottom of the sea, maybe, Mister Corbett.'

'If we must. But before that—could I not bid farewell? Could I not see my home once more? Could I not glimpse my children and my wife? A last look to bear away a bright image in the long dark wanderings to come?'

'But ain't you afraid they'll shriek and go distracted at the sight of you, Mister Corbett? For you're a grim object, sir—'

Though he tried to answer evenly and sensibly, his voice shook and broke with a new dismay.

'They'll not see me,' whispered the ghost. 'I'll peer through the parlour window. I'll not be seen. One last glimpse, I implore . . . so brief and to last for . . . so very long.'

'Through the window, then . . . the one at the back?'

Eagerly, the phantom nodded.

'And—and briefly?'

'Briefly!'

'You'll not betray?'

'Not I! Not I!'

It must have been half past midnight when they came to Gospel Oak, for all the houses but one were in darkness. The New Year had been born and safely cried out on the bells. No need to stay up longer. No harm would come to it now.

Benjamin Partridge and the ghost of his master moved cold and silent among the shadows where once they'd walked in the light. They crept towards the one house still awake.

The apothecary's shop stood halfway down the street, upon the right hand side. Candles shone from its windows, front and back. Mrs Corbett and her two children were awaiting the apothecary's return.

'They will be in the parlour,' murmured the apothecary's ghost, 'where I left them before . . . before—'

'Before what?' asked Benjamin dully.

'Before I left to bring you back,' whispered the ghost— and it was as if the words were torn from his thin substance with pain.

'To bring me back, Mister Corbett?'

'I was sorry to have sent you . . . on such a night. You spoke of pity. I was ashamed. I ran . . . and ran . . . and—'

The phantom's voice trailed away like a piece of drapery, caught in a carriage door, vanishing with a flutter in the speeding night.

It was now that Benjamin Partridge's soul began to groan and crack under the burden of the ghost. Fear, shame, and remorse are great weights to endure when there's no remedy.

★   ★   ★

'Alice!' whispered the ghost sadly. They were by the parlour window, concealed among such shadows as the leafless garden afforded.

Mrs Corbett—a plump, truly plain woman—sat by the fire, looking up from time to time as faint sounds made her think her husband was coming back.

'My love . . . my darling Alice,' sighed the phantom, for this dumpling of a lady was the ghost's dear darling. She was his love, his joy, the fire of his youth and the warmth of his middle life.

Her face was still smooth, though faint shadows crossed it, forerunners of that grief that would soon tear and crumple it when she should know of her husband's end. Unbearable grief—yet grief that would have to be borne.

Burning tears filled Benjamin Partridge's eyes and flowed, scalding, down his cheeks. What had he done? What had he done?

'Come—for pity's sake, come away!'

'My children . . .' whispered the ghost. 'A glimpse of them. A last glimpse—'

Two sons had Mister Corbett: one was eight and the other was rising five. They were no more remarkable to look on than was their mother as they sat by her side awaiting their father's return. They had fair hair and pink faces and sleepy looks about them, even though they'd been promised a New Year's present when their father should return. The older one did not look so much the older—even though he was now the family's head.

'Come away!' breathed Benjamin shakily, for the ghost was very close to the window, helplessly drawn by the sight within. Then—

'For God's sake—no! No!'

The youngest child had looked up. He'd heard something. A twig snapping under Benjamin's foot.

'Go back! Go back, Mister Corbett!'

Too late. The child had seen. Surprise and pleasure shone in his face.

'Papa!' he shouted. 'Look! Papa's in the garden! He's playing a game! He's hiding!'

In vain did their mother cry out that the air was cold and damp, that the hour was late, that their father would come in directly, directly. There was no stopping two such dancing children as they flew out into the garden on the saddest errand in all the world.

Their shouts and their laughter and the glimpses of their shining New Year faces were more terrible to Benjamin than all that had gone before. They were playing hide-and-seek with their father's ghost. Harsh beyond belief was this mockery of their innocence; monstrous beyond measure was this betrayal of their love.

'Papa! Where are you? Come back!'

They saw Benjamin. Shouted: 'Benjamin! Happy New Year! Come and help us catch Papa!'

But the apprentice crouched close to the ground, blinded by his tears.

'Papa!' shrieked the youngest on a dreadful sudden. 'I see you!'

The phantom, caught at last in the child's bright eyes, stood forlorn and still.

'Papa! The present—the present!'

What could the ghost give except terror and freezing cold? But the child was scarcely five and could not know that.

'No! No!' sobbed Benjamin, his proud heart and soul torn to shreds within him. The child was running with outstretched arms—in the way he'd run a thousand times before, and been caught up and swung high by his Papa.

'Papa! Where are you?'

'What have I done? What have I done?' moaned Benjamin Partridge; for the little boy had run and run— and passed through his father like air.

'It was a trick! One of your tricks, Papa—'

Bewildered, the child had stumbled and fallen. Now he stood up, chilled by he knew not what. Tears came into his eyes. 'Papa . . . where are you? Come back—'

But there was no one there. Despairingly, the apprentice and the phantom had fled as Mrs Corbett's voice called: 'Tom! Tom! Come in, dear! The children will take cold!'

Where now was there left to go? The street, only the empty street. But there was no escape. A coach was coming, casting its bright yellow light too far and too wide.

The apothecary's shop alone offered sanctuary, bitter though it was. The shop with its high mahogany counter behind which Benjamin Partridge and his ghost might crouch in their misery and their shame and hide, for a little while, from all the world. For the door to the parlour and beyond was ever closed to Mrs Corbett and her children. To the last, the apothecary had kept tenderness out of his daily sight.

But even this refuge was denied. The shop door opened. Footsteps crossed the floor. Sharp knuckles rapped on the wood above Benjamin's head.

'Benjamin Partridge! The mixture. You failed to deliver it!'

Benjamin stood up and stared at the New Year's first customer. Now he was tall and thin as a winter's tree and seemed to fill the shop from floor to ceiling—the terrible old man! His eyes burned with unnatural fire; but that might have been on account of his feverish cold.

Benjamin felt in his pockets. Found the undelivered jar. Then a desperate idea came to him. A frail hope . . .

'Sir . . . we . . . we only give j-jars in exchange. An empty jar, sir. Please . . . have you the . . . an empty jar? *Please?*'

'Do you mean *this* jar, Benjamin Partridge?' asked the old man, and held out the fatal jar with its knotted black ribbon.

From outside came the voices of Mrs Corbett and her children, searching in the garden. Already there was an edge to the unknowing widow's voice.

'The jar!' pleaded Benjamin. 'The jar!'

'What will you give me now, Benjamin Partridge? I'm not in business for my health, young man.'

'My heart and soul!' groaned Benjamin, believing at last that he'd done business with the Devil.

'Pooh!' said the old man contemptuously. 'A shifty bargain, that! To offer what ain't yours to give? It seems to me, Benjamin Partridge, that your heart and soul's been pretty heavily mortgaged already.'

'Then take my life, sir,' whispered the crushed apprentice, and prepared to take his last look at the living world which, at that time, consisted in the queer old man and the piteous apothecary's ghost.

'And have you haunt *me*, young man? Not yet . . . not yet.'

'Then there's no hope for . . . for them?' He looked towards the door that led to the family's home.

The old man did not answer. A fit of violent snuffles had overtaken him. Then he sneezed three or four times and sprayed the air with the result.

'You're lucky, young man, that I've got such a chill. In my younger days . . . in my younger days things would have been different. But I grow old. And these damp nights—'

Again he sneezed. 'So give me my mixture, Benjamin Partridge, and take back the empty jar. But,' he said, as Benjamin reached out with shaking hands, 'there'll still be something to pay for my trouble, young man. It was to have been a quarter of your life's earnings. Well, in the circumstances, we must make you an allowance, I suppose. Shall we say, a quarter of a week's earnings? Next week's? A quarter. I always work in quarters. Old habits—unlike apothecaries—die hard. That's fair, ain't it?'

'Agreed! Agreed!' cried Benjamin, who'd gladly have settled for a great deal more. 'When shall I pay?'

'You'll see,' said the old man, taking his precious mixture. 'It'll be when you least expect it.'

'The jar!' breathed Benjamin.

'The jar,' smiled the old man—and smashed it on the floor!

'Tom! Tom! What's wrong? Are you in the shop? Are you ill? Answer me!' came Mrs Corbett's voice on the other side of the door.

From long, hard habit, Benjamin reached for a brush and pan to sweep up the sharp fragments of glass.

'Good night, Benjamin Partridge,' murmured the old man mockingly. 'A happy New Year!'

Benjamin moved round to the front of the counter.

Mister Corbett's corpse lay at his feet. But where was the apothecary's ghost?

It was rising from behind the counter and smiling meekly, gently, gratefully. Then that poor, fearful, lonely, anxious, obliging phantom laid its hands on Benjamin's breast, nodded as if in confirmation of an interesting fact—and crept back towards its mortal shell. Slowly, slowly it sank, till it and the corpse were one. The fit was perfect. The ghost was gone.

'Tom! Tom! Please answer!' the door handle rattled; the door began to open . . .

'A happy New Year, Alice!' exclaimed Mister Corbett, rising uncertainly to his feet and rubbing his troubled head!

Loud rejoicing and wild cheerfulness were not in the nature of things for that night. Mrs Corbett and her two children did not—then or ever—know that Mister Corbett had come back from the dead. Instead, their chief pleasure was that Benjamin Partridge had been brought back to drink a health with them all by the family fire.

There was nothing remarkable in Mister Corbett's returning. Indeed, why should there be.

'We should have done this last year,' said Mrs Corbett, much touched by the tears of pleasure that stood in the apprentice's eyes.

'I . . . I would have,' murmured Mister Corbett, 'but I thought he was so anxious to be off—'

And, though Mister Corbett smiled in his old, old way, his apprentice could not restrain his tears of joy as he clasped his master's hand.

'A happy New Year, Mister Corbett!'

The hand was strong and, thank God, it was warm!

Suddenly he began to wonder if his dark adventure had been a dream. The thought—the hope, even—took root and grew strong. When Mister Corbett offered, indeed, insisted on taking him home in his own carriage, the hope had become all but a certainty. The Apprentice's Dream. That's what it had been. The Apprentice's Dream of his Master's Ghost. No more than that—

'By the way, Master Partridge,' said Mister Corbett as they rattled towards Kentish Town. 'Did you deliver that mixture?'

'Yes indeed, sir,' said Benjamin uneasily.

'Did the old fellow pay you?'

'I . . . I forgot to ask, sir . . .'

Mister Corbett chuckled. 'Never mind, Master Partridge. But I'll have to take it from your wages next week, my boy. It'll be—' He paused and rubbed his head as if trying to remember something. 'Shall we say a quarter of your next week's wages? We must start the New Year right!'

Benjamin's composure suffered a very sharp set-back, and it was not till they reached Mrs Partridge's—an hour after midnight, but welcome none the less—and had sat and drunk healths and 'happy New Years' in the firelight and candlelight, that Benjamin's heart began to beat evenly once more.

'My son is lucky to have you for a master, Mister Corbett,' declared Mrs Partridge cheerfully.

'And I'm lucky to have him for an apprentice,' said Mister Corbett courteously, but with an air of meaning it.

Then Mrs Partridge and Mister Corbett were both surprised and touched by the strength and passion of Benjamin's agreement.

'Lucky?' he cried. 'Lucky? Oh yes, indeed we are!'

For, though he'd studied Mister Corbett as hard as he could, against every manner and source of light, he'd not been able to see through him at all!

But what he had been able to see was a world restored. All its skies, seasons, fruits, and joys—all days, nights, friends, and pleasant evenings—were back with him once more.

And what he could see also—even then and for ever after, for such things once seen are never forgot—was that obliging, anxious, and oddly touching ghost, dwelling in its mansion of flesh: Mister Corbett's soul.

Each time he stared into Mister Corbett's eyes—which he did from time to time when there passed a sharpness between him and his master—he saw that ghost again . . . Then he smiled, and Mister Corbett smiled as he, too, half remembered a strange adventure between them, on New Year's Eve.

2
VAARLEM AND TRIPP

VAARLEM AND TRIPP

I t's certain he has a great gift: but otherwise he is a very contemptible, vile little man—strong-smelling, even, and well known in the Amsterdam courts for fraud, embezzlement, and bankruptcy. It's very humiliating to be his pupil, but, as my father says, if God has planted a lily in a cesspit, one must stop up one's nose and go down. Of late, my task has been to choose his brushes, pigment, and canvas. He tells me this is as important a part of the craft of painting as there is, but the truth of the matter is that he's so much in debt and disgrace that he daren't show his face outside the studio. My name is Roger Vaarlem; my master is Joseph Tripp, of course.

A month ago he was before the burghers who told him his portrait of the admiral was unacceptable— insulting, even—and demanded their advance of guilders back. Having spent it, he offered to paint the admiral again, but was not trusted: and rightly. Truth to Nature was one thing (no one could deny the portrait had a deal of truth in it, for my master has his gift), but truth to one's country and employers must come first. So he was given the opportunity of redeeming himself by painting a grand battle-piece to be hung in the Town Hall. Or prosecution in the courts again. Angrily (he told me) he accepted, and was granted a cabin aboard the *Little Willelm*. We sailed at half past eight this morning.

Though the early morning had been warm and brilliant, he was muffled in every garment he could find, careless of their cleanliness, which is a strong point aboard Dutch ships. It was very shameful to be walking along beside him, carrying his sketchbooks and other belongings which smelled worse than the tar and pickled fish with which the air was strong. There were two ships of ninety guns nodding in a stately fashion upon the gentle tide: cathedrals of gilded wood with triple spires and delicate crosses, netted and festooned like for a Saint's Day. The thought crossed my mind of parting from Mynheer Tripp and going to sea on my own, but my father would have prosecuted him for negligence and fraud and he'd have gone to gaol for it.

Then we came to the *Little Willelm* and he at once began to complain that it was insufficiently armed and pointed out the maze of stitching on the fore-topsail where English musket-fire had peppered it to a sieve. Together with all his other qualities, he is a great coward and I felt myself blush as he ranted on in the hearing of one of the ship's officers. Then, with my hand to his elbow, he went aboard, stepping down on the deck as if it were a single floating plank and not secure.

The *Little Willelm*, being but a smallish barquentine, could offer only a tiny cabin next to the surgeon's; but at least it was clean which flattered Mynheer Tripp unwarrantably.

'Go away, Vaarlem!' he mumbled, and crawled on to the bunk—for the motion of the ship at its moorings was already unsettling his stomach. So I left him and went out on to the maindeck in the sunny air and watched the crew go about their business in the rigging and on the yards.

'How come a fine-looking lad like you goes about with an old rag-bag like him?'

Mynheer Leyden—an officer of good family—was standing by me.

I answered: 'Sir—he's a great man, whatever you may think, and will be remembered long after you and me are forgot.'

After all, one has one's pride!

Mynheer Leyden would have answered, but Captain Kuyper began shouting from the quarter-deck to cast off and Mynheer Leyden shrugged his smooth shoulders and went about his duties. These seemed to consist in putting his hands behind his back and pacing the larboard rail, nodding to the crowd of fishwives and early clerks who always throng the harbour in the mornings to watch the glorious ships heave and puff out their sails like proud white chests and lean their way into the dangerous sea.

Once out of the harbour, the foresail was set and I went below to inform Mynheer Tripp he was missing a very wonderful sight, for there was not much wind and the great spread of canvas seemed to be but breathing against invisible, creaking stays. But he was already up and about—and in a more cheerful mood. He'd had intelligence that the *Little Willelm* was to sail west by south-west to lure enemy vessels into pursuit, when they'd be blown out of the water by our own great ships which would be following on the next tide. His cheerfulness arose from the discovery that the *Little Willelm* was the swiftest vessel in the Channel and was not intended to fight.

'A clean pair of heels, eh? Ha-ha!' he kept saying . . . and grinning in a very unwholesome manner. It was the only time I'd ever known him take a real pleasure in cleanliness. Later on, his spirits rose high enough for him to behave in his usual way. He began soliciting guilders from the officers to portray them prominently in the battle-piece. Full of shame—for he was earning a good deal of contempt—I warned him he'd be prosecuted for false pretences.

'Why?' he muttered angrily—the wind catching the soft brim of his black hat and smacking his face with it.

'Because they won't be larger than thumb-nails, sir!'

'You mind your own business, Vaarlem!' he snarled, quite beside himself where guilders were concerned. 'If those little tinsel nobodies tell their dough-faced relatives that such and such blob of paint is their darling—well? Why not? What's wrong with a little family pride? Immortal, that's what they'll be! So keep your middle-class nose out of my affairs, Master Vaarlem . . . or I'll paint you as an Englishman!'

He stalked away, holding his hat with one hand and his filthy shawls and oil-stained coat with the other. But soon after, he sidled back again and remarked ingratiatingly, 'No need to tell your papa everything I say, Roger, dear lad . . . words spoke in haste . . . no need for misunderstandings; eh? Dear boy . . .'

He was so mean, he was frightened my father would withdraw me as his pupil—and with me would go guilders. I looked at him coldly, while he bit his lip and brooded uneasily on whether he'd cut off his nose to spite his face; not that either would have been the loser.

I was more offended than I cared to let him know, so I obliged by keeping my nose out of his affairs for the remainder of the day. Which wasn't difficult, as he kept to the great cabin with the surgeon. Not that he was really ill—God forbid!—but he was cunningly picking the surgeon's wits relative to every ache and pain that plagued him. While all the while, the simple surgeon was happily imagining himself in the forefront of the Town Hall's battle-piece, a hero for ever. (Mynheer Tripp did indeed make a small sketch of him: a very wonderful piece of work—for somehow he caught a look of bewilderment and embarrassment in the surgeon's eyes as if God had too often stared them out.)

I'd intended to leave him for much longer than I did; at one time in the day I'd very serious thoughts indeed of leaving him altogether and fighting for Holland. This was when we saw our first English sail and there was great activity on the lower gun-deck against the chance of an encounter. She was a handsome, warlike vessel, bosoming strongly along. 'A seventy-four,' remarked Mynheer Leyden briskly. 'By tomorrow she'll be driftwood!' Then we outpaced her and the sea was as clean as a German silver tray.

It was a few minutes before half past eight o'clock in the evening. I'd been on deck together with several officers. The wind was gone. The air was still. A sharp-edged quarter moon seemed to have sliced the clouds into strips, so that they fell away slowly, leaving dark threads behind. Earlier, Mynheer Leyden had been urging me to speak with the captain relative to my becoming a midshipman, for I was of good family and too good for Mynheer Tripp. To be a painter was a lower-class ambition. ('All right! He has his gift! But what's that to you and me? God gave him sharp eyes—but He gave us good families! Vaarlem, my boy—I can't make you out!') Then, a few minutes before half past eight, he said quietly, 'Vaarlem: you'd best go down and fetch him.' Which I did.

'Sir: you must come up on deck at once.'

Mynheer Tripp glanced at me irritably, began to mumble something, then thought better of it. He stood up and wrapped himself in the filthy shawls and coat he'd strewn about the cabin.

'Hurry, sir!'

'Why? The sea won't run away . . . and if it does, I shan't be sorry!' He followed me on to the deck.

'Look, Mynheer Tripp! The Englishman!'

For a proud moment, I thought he'd had enough brandy to make him behave like a Dutchman, for he stood quite still and silent. Then the brandy's effect wore off and his own miserable spirit shone through. Every scrap of colour went from his face and he began to tremble with terror and rage!

'Madmen!' he shrieked—and I wished myself at the

bottom of the sea and Mynheer Tripp with me. The
Englishman was within half a kilometre, and still moving
softly towards us, pulled by two longboats whose oars
pricked little silver buds in the moonswept sea. She was as
silent as the grave, and any moment now would turn,
broadside on, and greet us with the roar of thirty-seven
iron mouths. For she was the seventy-four.

Mynheer Tripp seized my arm and began dragging
me towards the quarter-deck, shouting outrageously:
'Move off! For God's sake move off! We'll all be killed!
How dare you do such a thing! Look! Look! This boy . . .
of a good family . . . very important! If he's harmed I'll
be prosecuted by his father. And so will you! I demand to
go back! For Vaarlem's sake! Oh, my God! A battle!'

They must have heard him aboard the Englishman. I
could only pray that no one aboard it knew Dutch! I felt
myself go as red as a poppy. To be used by this villainous
coward as a mean excuse—I all but fought with him!

'You pig, Mynheer Tripp!' I panted. 'This time you've
gone too far!'

'Pig?' he hissed, between roarings at the captain. 'You
shut your middle-class mouth, Master Vaarlem! These
noodles have no right to expose me . . . us to such danger!
I'll sue—that's what I'll do! In the courts!'

Captain Kuyper—a man who'd faced death a hundred
times and now faced it for maybe the last—stared at
Mynheer Tripp as if from a great distance.

'You are perfectly right, sir. This ship is no place for
you. You will be put off in the boat and rowed to where
you may observe the engagement in safety. Or go to
Holland. Or go to Hell, sir! As for the boy—he may stay
if he chooses. I would not be ashamed to die in *his*
company.'

To my astonishment, before I could answer—and
God knows what I'd have said—Mynheer Tripp burst out
with: 'How dare you, sir, put such ideas into a boy's head!

What d'you expect him to say? A boy of good family like him! Unfair, sir! Cruel! Dishonest! What can he know? I warn you, if you don't put him off, I'll not stir from your miserable ship! Both of us—or none! Oh, there'll be trouble! In the courts!'

Then he turned his mean, inflamed face towards me and muttered urgently: 'Keep quiet, Vaarlem! None of your business! Don't you dare say a word! I forbid it!'

Captain Kuyper shrugged his shoulders and turned away. 'Put them both in the boat, and let one man go with them to take the oars. Immediately! I want Mynheer Tripp off this ship at once. Or by God, I'll throw him off!'

Quite sick with shame, I followed Mynheer Tripp, who'd scuttled to the boat and hopped into it, clutching his sketchbooks and horrible clothes about him—in a panic that the captain would do him a mischief.

The sailor who rowed us was a tall, silent fellow by the name of Krebs. For about twenty minutes he said nothing but rowed with a seemingly slow, but steady stroke. Mynheer Tripp, his head hunched into his shoulders, grasped my wrist and stared at the diminishing bulk of the *Little Willelm* which lay between us and the huge Englishman. Implacably, the Englishman came nearer and nearer and still did not turn. We could no more see the longboats . . . but the men in them must have had nerves of iron, for they were within musket range of the *Little Willelm* and could have been shot to pieces.

'Faster! Faster!' urged my master, as the bowsprit of the Englishman appeared to nod above the *Willelm*'s deck. There looked to be no more than fifty metres between them. Then she began to slew round . . . ponderously . . . malignantly . . .

'Will you watch from here, sirs?' Krebs had stopped rowing. There was nothing contemptuous in the way he spoke. He simply wanted to know.

'Is it . . . is it safe?'

Krebs eyed the distance. 'Most likely . . . yes, sir.'

The two ships now lay side by side—the Englishman's aft projecting beyond the *Willelm*. Her after-castle, much gilded and gleaming under three lanterns, rose nearly as high as the *Willelm*'s mizzen yard. A very unequal encounter. Perhaps she thought so? And was waiting for a surrender?

Krebs shipped his oars and stuck his chin in his great hands. Calmly he stared at the dark shape of his own ship, outlined against the sombre, spiky brown of her enemy. Though the shrouds and yards must have been alive with marksmen, nothing stirred to betray them.

'Thank God we ain't aboard!' he remarked at length. Mynheer Tripp nodded vigorously. He'd begun to make sketches by the light of a small lantern. Approvingly, Krebs glanced at them. Very workmanlike. I began to feel cold and lonely. Was I the only one who wished himself back aboard the *Little Willelm*?

The beginnings of a breeze. The great ghostly sails of the Englishman began to shift, but not quite to fill. The *Willelm*'s sails being smaller, bellied out more fatly. The bold little Dutchman and the skinny Englishman began to move. Masts, which had seemed all of one ship, began to divide—to part asunder . . .

There seemed to be a moment of extraordinary stillness—even breathlessness—when suddenly a huge yellow flower of fire grew out of the side of the Englishman. (Beautiful Dutch lady—take my murdering bouquet!)

And then enormous billows of reddish smoke roared and blossomed up, blundering through the rigging and fouling the sails and sky. The engagement was begun.

A faint sound of screaming and shouting reached us, but was instantly drowned in the roar of the *Willelm*'s broadside. Then the Englishman fired again—this time

with grapeshot, which makes an amazing, shrieking sound as it flies.

'The mainmast! D'you see? They've got the mainmast!' muttered Krebs, his face white even in the reddish glare of the encounter. 'Shrouds and halyards cut through—murder, for them on deck! Slices them in two and three parts! Murder, it is!'

The *Willelm* was still firing—but not full broadsides. Half her ports must have been shattered.

'They've got to heave the dead out of the way!' Krebs said very urgently—as if it was his immediate task. 'Can't get to the powder quick enough with all them dead tangling up the trunnions . . . got to heave 'em out . . . Cap'n'll be down there now—he'll be doing the right thing—'

Another flash and roar from the Englishman: not so vast as the first. Was she disabled, too?

'Quarter-deck cannon,' mumbled Krebs, suddenly

scowling. 'Now you'll see—' Again, she roared. 'Upper
deck cannon . . . fourteen killers there!' A third blaze and
roar. Krebs nodded. 'Lower-deck. They know what
they're at. Give no chance . . . no chance at all . . .'

The *Willelm* seemed to have stopped firing. 'Look!
Poor devils up in the cross-trees. D'ye see? Firebrands!
Nought else left! But they'll never reach to the
Englishman. Poor devils! Oh, God! She's afire herself!
Keep your heads down, sirs! She'll be going up in a
minute! A-ah!'

Even as he spoke, the fire must have reached the
Willelm's powder store. There was a glare and a
thunderous crackling sound like the end of the world—as
indeed for many it was. With a shriek of terror, Mynheer
Tripp—who'd been extraordinarily absorbed throughout
the encounter, oblivious to everything but his rapid, intent
drawing—flung himself to the bottom of the boat: a
quaking bundle of disgusting rags. Then the great light
went out of the sky and the air was full of smoke and the
sharp, bitter smell of spent powder and burnt out lives.
Pieces of wood began to kiss the water about us. When at
last the smoke drifted up to the moon, we saw the guilty
hump of the Englishman sliding away, leaving nothing
more behind than a torn-up patch of sea, rough with
driftwood and darknesses.

'Oh, God! Now what's to become of us?' wept
Mynheer Tripp. I begged him to be quiet, for things were
bad enough without his assistance. Krebs had been hit in
the neck by a flying piece of iron and was bleeding like a
pig. If he wasn't bandaged, he'd die. Mynheer Tripp
plucked at one of his shawls—not offering it, but
indicating that, if pressed, he'd part with it. It was filthy
enough to have killed Krebs outright: by poisoning. There
was nothing for it but to use my shirt; which I did,
watched by Mynheer Tripp who snarled when I tore it
into strips:

'I hope you know that was your best linen, Vaarlem!'

Which mean remark did nothing but gain me unnecessary thanks from Krebs who could scarcely speak: his wound having severed a tendon and opened a great vessel. He lay in the bottom of the boat while I took the oars, watched by that dirty jelly in the stern. All I could see of Mynheer Tripp were his miserably reproachful eyes.

'You'll die of cold,' he mumbled furiously.

'*I* can keep warm by rowing, sir!' I said, hoping to shame him. I pulled towards the *Little Willelm*'s grave in the frail hope of survivors, but found none. Then, under Kreb's whispered directions, I began to row eastward, into the path of our hoped-for followers on the coming tide. But, being no craftsman of oars, we did little more than drift in that dark and hostile sea: Mynheer Tripp, Krebs, and me. For two or even three hours . . . As Mynheer Tripp had predicted, it was violently cold. I began to shiver and sweat at the same time. My hands were growing very sore and swollen. When I paused to shift my grip, I found them to be bleeding; and Mynheer Tripp, without once stopping, moaned and cursed the sea and the murdering Englishman. Which served no purpose at all. But then he's not the best of companions in such circumstances. He hates the sea and can't abide the sight of blood. Also, there are a million other things capable of panicking him. The chief problem is to avoid being infected by this.

At about one o'clock the breeze began to blow more briskly and in a changed direction. Long bands of cloud began to shift and obscure the moon. The darkness grew thick and formidable; Mynheer Tripp's eyes were no longer visible—but I felt their continuing reproach. Krebs was quite silent and, every now and again, I thought he'd died and had to stop rowing to put my head to his chest and be greeted with: 'Still here . . . don't you worry . . . keep it up, boy—' So back I'd go to my task, abysmally

cold and frightened, but not wanting to give the odious
Mynheer Tripp the opportunity for gloating.

Then I thought we were saved! Lanterns glinted high
up in the night ahead. Our ships at last! I shouted and
waved the dim remains of our lantern. Krebs struggled up
on his elbow. He said, 'It's the Englishman again!'

'Douse the light, Vaarlem!' shrieked Mynheer Tripp.
But it was too late. We'd been seen. The Englishman
hailed us.

'Ahoy, there!' Which, in Dutch, means, 'Stand fast or
we'll pepper you with musket-fire!'

Nearer and nearer she came, a glinting, ghostly monster.
Mynheer Tripp began to gabble we'd be tortured and
hanged. I never felt more ashamed of him in my life. He was
quaking with terror. I sweated to think of how the English
would sneer . . . a craven Dutchman. Maybe I could swear
he was French: or German? The great ship was alongside.
The murderous cannon still poked out of their ports like
blunt black teeth against the dark sky. Two English sailors
came down on ropes and hoisted Krebs between them. I was
surprised by how like Dutchmen they looked. We were
bidden to follow, when Mynheer Tripp further disgraced
our nation by being frightened of falling off the rope.

'For God's sake, sir!' I hissed at him. 'Make a good
showing.'

'What d'you mean, "for God's sake", Vaarlem?' he
hissed back. 'You nasty little prig!'

With much contemptuous laughter, more sailors came
and helped Mynheer Tripp up between them. I followed
on my own. No sooner was I on deck than Mynheer
Tripp—who'd got a considerable, jeering crowd about
him, shouted in his bad English: 'Cover him up! Boy of
good family, that! He'll die of cold!' I flushed angrily, but
a huge cloth was brought and wrapped round me. To
my indignation, I saw it was an English flag. I stripped it
off and flung it down.

'I'd *rather* die of cold than be covered with that!' I meant to display *some* Dutch spirit and show we weren't all like Mynheer Tripp.

'Brave lad!' said an officer—the captain, I think. 'Worthier than his companion, eh? What say we heave the old fellow back?'

I grew alarmed. Begged them to do no such thing. 'Though you may not think it, he's a great man . . . greater than all of us put together!'

'A greater coward, you mean, boy! How come you go about with such a rag-bag?'

But fortunately, Mynheer Tripp hadn't heard the threat. He was by the mizzen-mast lantern, examining his drawings to see they were intact. A number of officers and sailors were staring over his shoulder. Then more and more came, with more lanterns, lighting up that patch of deck which seemed roofed with canvas and walled by the netted shrouds. Krebs and his honourable wound, and myself and my defiance were left and forgotten. A greater victory was in the making. Of a sudden, I began to feel very proud to be Mynheer Tripp's pupil, and my eyes kept filling with tears on that account. I picked up the flag and wrapped out the cold with it, and went to join the English crowd about my master. Krebs, feeling stronger, leaned on me and stared.

Not all the ships and cannon and defiance in the world could have done what he'd done. With a few lines—no more—he'd advanced into the enemies' hearts and set up his flag there. Mynheer Tripp's victory had been with God's gift—not with the gunsmith's. It's a mercy, I suppose, he never really knew his own power—else he'd have suffocated it under guilders. The Englishmen stared at the drawings, then, seeing Krebs, began comparing with him—in slow English and bad Dutch—the terror and grandeur of their experience, so uncannily caught by the sniffing and shuffling Mynheer Tripp. Pennants, flags, even countries were forgotten. An aspect of battle was seen with neither Dutch nor English eyes, but with a passion and a pity that encompassed all.

'Mynheer Tripp,' said the English captain—a handsome, well-bred man, most likely of Dutch descent, 'you are a very great man. We are honoured. As our guest, sir, I invite you to visit England.'

My master looked at me—not with pride or any so respectable a thing, but with his usual greed and cunning. He said, in his horrible English, 'Good! Good! I will paint your admiral, maybe—?'

And then to me in Dutch, with an offensive smirk: 'You see, Vaarlem, these English are different. I told you so. I'll be appreciated—not prosecuted. Just wait till they see what I make of *their* admiral! Money back, indeed! And after all, my boy, guineas is as good as guilders, eh? He-he!'

He really is the most contemptible man I know! I wonder what the English will make of him: and what he'll make of the English?

3
THE SIMPLETON

CHAPTER ONE

In the year 1749, on January the eighteenth at Lewes Assizes, my old friend Nicholas Kemp collected seven years' transportation and a sermon from the judge as long as a monkey's arm.

Poor Nick! He stood there in the dock, his happy young face all bewildered when the jury brought in their verdict, and the judge said better men had been hanged for less.

Every advantage, the judge declared he'd had: meaning his family being in a good way of trade (if you care for such things), and as respectable as a church pew.

'But in spite of everything, you've turned out a bad lot, Master Kemp.'

Here, Nick looked honestly depressed and surprised that anyone should think so ill of him. Which was a trifle impudent, we thought. After all, he'd only been fourteen when he'd left his home under a cloud—and I don't mean the sort that makes up weather!

He'd prigged some trinkets from his father's workshop (his father being a silversmith), and given them to some flighty doxy of twelve or thereabouts. Yes indeed, if Nick had one weakness above all others, it was for a pretty face. It wasn't a weakness like yours or mine which stays with a wink and a laugh and a kiss and a cuddle; it was a real sighing bog of a weakness. Believe me or not, he was one of your moonfaced lovers who twang and twiddle outside ladies' windows till someone empties a chamberpot on them to keep them quiet.

On this, his first mistake, he'd been unlucky enough to pick on the daughter of the trinkets' lawful owner—who took offence and worse. Nick left that very night, with his heart, I'm sure, carved on a dozen trees.

'If I didn't think there was some goodness in your soul,' went on the judge, 'I'd have you hanged out of hand.'

Well, well—he was a judge and had had his bellyful of human nature. If he saw goodness in Nick's soul, it must have been there.

'So it's seven years in Virginia for you, Nicholas Kemp,' finished up the judge. 'And may you be improved by it.'

Nick gave a great sigh and looked as glum and heart-broken as if the hangman had asked for his neck.

'Poor soul!' muttered someone at the back. 'I'd have sworn he was innocent.'

Which was exactly what Nick *had* sworn—till he'd been peached on by the rosy-cheeked trollop he'd birthday'd with a silver watch he'd prigged the previous morning. We'd warned him she was a low-class slut; but, not being exactly a gentleman himself, he'd no yardstick to judge her by. Even got peeved and told us to be content with the guineas he'd passed on and leave the watch to him. She was one of Nature's ladies, he said, and had promised not to wear the watch for a fortnight.

It was a large watch, as I remember it: a shade vulgar, like Nick. She wore it as soon as his back was turned—and in the parlour of the White Horse, which was where it had been prigged. Need I say more?

A peace officer with a neck like a bull came to our lodgings. Nick shot under the table.

'Ad we any notion of a young 'un called Kemp? If so, it were oor dooty to give 'im up.

I ask you—what could we do? Nick looked a trifle put out, at first, but then took it in good part when we reminded him we'd told him so. I fancy he knew where the blame really lay. Lord! You should have seen the look he hung on that trollop when she gave her evidence! Stones would have wept. (Though, I must admit, we couldn't resist a chuckle.) But jurors' hearts are made of sterner stuff . . .

So we took a coach down to Deal to see him off. The *Phoenix* out of Deptford was anchored there, dipping and bobbing like an enormous bridesmaid, all laced and gilded and wanting only her fat bodice and petticoat to be put on that she might billow out to some roaring wedding at sea.

But she wasn't the doxy after Nick's heart, and his face was as long as a coffin when he shuffled, leg-ironed, into the rowboat with half a dozen assorted embezzlers, pickpockets, and ragged layabouts, all Virginia bound.

We waved, but I don't think he saw us, so we left it till next morning when we hired a fisherman to row us out to the *Phoenix* to send our poor friend off in convivial style.

A tremendous great brute of a ship was the *Phoenix*— when we got close—and as far past her prime as was reasonable with still being afloat. She creaked and grunted and groaned even in the calm waters, so what she would do when the wind blew, God and her captain alone knew.

But there was no sense or kindness in frightening poor Nick, so we all toasted him in gin and drank to the teeming doxies in Virginia—far fairer than our English drabs—and kept to ourselves the belief he'd not make halfway over with his soul and body in one piece.

I don't know whether he was still in irons then, for we could only see his head and shoulders poking out of a gun port, six feet aloft.

'Cheer up, Nick!' one of us shouted. 'There's a Richmond in Virginia with a lass that's peach to porridge to the blowsy damsel here!'

But he looked as if his silly heart would break.

'Cheer up, Nick!' I roared. 'Gentlemen pay fifty pound for a trip like yours!'

I think he was going to smile. He'd a fair sense of humour—which was part of the reason we kept his acquaintance, that and his skill in keeping us in funds— yes, I'm sure he was going to smile when another convict poked his head out beside him and spat mightily into the sea; so we all had to duck to avoid.

'Friends of your'n, sonny?' asked this fellow curiously, but poor Nick never answered a word. His heart was too full, we guessed.

So, 'Cheer up, Nick!' shouted the last of us. 'You're real lucky, you know! After all, as the good judge said, you might have been nubbed, old dear! For you wasn't exactly innocent, was you, Nick? Ha-ha!'

It was then that he spoke.

'Aye,' he said, in that rich voice of his that was always so surprising. 'I wan't innocent, was I? Not like you, friends.'

'What d'you mean, Nick?'

'Just what I say, *friends*.'

The privation in that stinking hold was having its effect on him, all right. It's always said that, put a mouse with rats and it grows sharper teeth and a longer tail. He leaned on *friends* very verminously indeed. We were all sorry to note it.

'You could have saved me, friends. You needn't have given me up.'

'Come along, Nick! Would you have us be accessories? We'd have been took along with you! And what would our families have said to that? Besides, I'm sure your feet was poking out of the table. And anyways, it was on account of the watch. Remember? We warned you. It was the watch that did it. And we'd no part in that, my lad!'

'No,' said Nick, somewhat sourly for him. 'Your hands were clean. For once.'

A nasty dig, that. But we all made allowances, I think. We didn't want to show bitterness to a friend in distress.

So we smiled and toasted him again and gave the boatman the nod to pull away. No sense in drawing out what had turned so sour . . .

Then, as we began to shift off, he shouted after us, 'I may be a scapegoat, friends—but there's some sins I'll not carry off for you! There's some sins that'll always come home to roost!'

Here was an unchristian sentiment if ever there was one! In what Scripture, for God's sake, does the scapegoat turn round and snarl? Something devilish there.

None the less, we kept our charity and drank Nick's salvation deep into the night, remembering good times together and ending up quite merry. I speak no less than the truth when I say we all had a warm corner in our hearts for that simpleton, Nicholas Kemp. We forgave his turning on us and put it down to the ugly circumstance of his confinement, rather than to a nature grown unsteady.

Next morning, which was the twenty-first and Wednesday, we rose at ten and went down to the frontage of the sea, warmly meaning to row out once more and let bygones be bygones and give poor Nick a second chance to carry a gentle thought of us all into the hereafter.

But alas! It was not to be. The *Phoenix* had already spread her grubby finery and lumbered out to sea. When she was pointed out to us, she was no bigger than a thumbnail. We waved—and I recall our eyes grew moist with staring.

'The last of Nick Kemp,' sighed one of us. 'Let's go drink to his memory. Let's not forget he served us well, and, in his simple way, was faithful. But now he's gone, and I fancy the world's seen the end of him. Poor old Nick!'

'We'll not forget you, Nick,' I said, in sentimental mood. Never let it be said that your lack of breeding spoiled the goodness of your heart.'

'Farewell, Nick Kemp,' murmured the last of us, solemnly. 'Though the sea will most likely gobble up you and the dingy *Phoenix* in a day, I fancy, you'll live on in our hearts. It'll be many a long while before we find another such dear simple soul to take your place. So come, lads! Let's start looking!'

CHAPTER TWO

C ontrary to the confident expectations of the kind friends who'd seen him off, a day had passed and Nicholas Kemp was still alive and the *Phoenix* still afloat; though when the wind blew and the sea heaved, the groaning of the ship and the convicts together was such as to make any man think the end of the world was nigh.

Eighty-two of them slept, rolled, moaned, stank, and swore between the main- and fore-masts, on what had once been the lower gun deck. But the thirty-two pounders were gone, and out of the gun ports now, instead of ball and grapeshot, flew ancient hats, shrieks, old boots, bellows of song, bottles with painful messages, rats, pewter plates, and stinking pots to litter the old sea in a long, dancing line.

The convicts were a quarrelsome lot, having come from four stone prisons into this wooden one. And each of these prisons, which were Newgate, Marshalsea, the Fleet, and Lewes, had printed a fierce and rank comradeship on its own platoon. Thus the Newgate gentry jeered at the Marshalsea, who spat on the Fleet, who in their turn, did what they could to make life more wretched than it need have been for the six from Lewes Gaol.

Yet this last sturdy little band stood up remarkably well and gave as good as it took, or, rather, took somewhat more than was taken from it: thieving being as common as breathing and Sussex thieves being the busiest of all.

None the less, small as it was, even this band carried its passenger; one who was among them, so to speak, but not of them. One whose heart had fallen further than his boots and was languishing over a large part of Southern England,

carved into trees, scratched on to doors, marked up in ale
on tavern windows and, once, painted in blood (thinly—
from a scratch) on an alderman's coach. Nicholas Kemp
crouched lost in his tender past. While round about him the
profoundest activities went on, he mooned away in his
private night, where the stars were bright, bright eyes.

Yet there must have been something about him that
touched even the hardest heart. No one kicked him; no
one trod on him; no one clouted him round the head.
Instead, to his great surprise, he found himself in the midst
of a kind of plenty. Tattered blankets and stolen dinners
were passed stealthily on with a: 'Take it son. It's going
begging.'

These gifts from a darker heaven, so to speak, began
to fall soon after the ramshackle commotion on deck
declared the *Phoenix* to be under way and the wind set fair
for Virginia.

First a neckerchief and then a pair of mittens were
dropped in his lap.

'Put 'em on, sonny, afore you catch your death of
cold.'

Later came a smelly waistcoat.

'Roll it up, sonny. 'Twill serve as a pillow.'

Most gratefully (gratitude being another of his
weaknesses) Nick looked up, and a pair of beady eyes
looked briefly—almost contemptuously—down. Nicholas
Kemp, amiable soul that he was, seemed to have brought
out the father in a squat fierce embezzler called
Bartleman.

He was much moved by this strange circumstance,
and it served to calm his confused and agitated thoughts
concerning the three kind friends whose miserable
cowardice and stinking treachery had put him where he
was. Anger against himself for having been taken in and
against them for having done the taking, had contended
almost equally in his troubled mind.

He confided as much to Bartleman during the first pitchy night out of Deal, and felt easier in his mind for it.

'How'd you like to slit their throats, son?' came the embezzler's harsh voice. Then, before Nicholas could reply one way or the other, came a laugh that had a very fatal ring to it.

Disquieting as was this laugh, the next day brought a blanket and a pipe and enough 'son's' and 'sonny's' to furnish a madman's sky.

On this second day, which turned out to be brisk and blowy and laid half the convicts low, Bartleman's example inspired another of the Lewes company to pass on to Nicholas a quarter bottle of gin. Bartleman was formidably angry. He snatched up the bottle and bade the giver leave the lad to him. On which Nicholas felt uneasily that Bartleman had bought him, lock, stock, and barrel as a receptacle for his own charity.

Later that day came an incident even more striking. It had to do with the pipe. Though not much of a smoker (he preferred snuff when he could get it), Nicholas found there was some comfort to be had from sucking at the pipe while he squatted and contemplated the rusting iron of his fetters. The flavour of the tobacco brought back memories of inns and taverns. The memory of a tavern brought back the memory of a pair of cherry lips and hair like a fold of the night: his last heart-break. Though she'd helped to betray him, he forgave her with a sigh . . .

'Bleeding thief,' came a voice, thick with reproach. He looked up. Before him stood a bony, hideous ruffian from the Marshalsea company. He'd shuffled up unheard; there was such a grinding and clinking and clawing of leg-irons that all motions turned out stealthy—their sounds being swallowed up in the general uproar.

'Thief?' said Nicholas, reddening awkwardly. His accuser's fists were large, and roughened from easy use.

'You got my pipe, ain't you? You prigged it yesterday
and left me in a very pitiable state, mister. I been through
a horrible night on your account. I twitched and groaned
and me poor mouth felt like old leather. And now I sees
you, rosy as the bleeding dawn and a-smoking of my pipe
like it was your very own. You done wrong, mister, and
I'm a-going to beat you into pulp for it.'

'I—I found it,' attempted Nicholas, never having been
remarkable for his quickness in inventing excuses. He
smiled hopefully, then feebly, then not at all as he saw
he'd had no luck.

So he began to shrink backward, praying that he was
somehow in the grip of a nightmare from which he'd
shortly awaken and find himself a thousand miles away.

But no such awakening came. The nightmare went on
apace. Though well made and tolerably sturdy, he lacked
a fierce nature. Violence dismayed him. The Marshalsea
ruffian frightened the wits out of him.

Abruptly, he found himself hard against a bulkhead. He must have travelled six yards on his shaking bottom, with the monster coming on. Fifteen or twenty bleary faces regarded him with interest. None with compassion.

'Oh God,' whispered Nicholas, thinking he ought to be putting his affairs in order, for the Marshalsea man had hold of a short length of timber, studded with nails.

'God help me . . . God help me . . .' he went on, being no richer in prayer than he was in excuses. 'God help—'

'The lad said he found it, friend.'

Irritably, the Marshalsea man turned aside. Bartleman was there. Bartleman was grinning. Horrible sight. He had sharp, rat-like teeth.

'The lad said he found it, friend,' repeated Bartleman. 'And if you don't take his word, I'll cut your throat out. So help me, I will.'

Bartleman continued to grin. He had a knife, and it was plain he'd be happy to use it.

Much surprised, the Marshalsea man peered at Bartleman, and then to his one-time supporters. They looked absorbed . . . as if they'd never seen a throat cut before.

He licked his lips with a venomous rapidity and began to shuffle sideways, seeking to make a circle about the squat embezzler. But his leg-irons dragged on him, giving his motions the air of a tipsy country dance.

Amiably, Bartleman watched him: even seemed sympathetic.

'Them bracelets is cruel when you're over-size, friend. Which you should have thought on afore you came accusing sonny here.'

'I got no quarrel with you, mister,' said the Marshalsea man, not pausing in his circling.

Nicholas stared at his champion with gloomy uncertainty. Bartleman was the smaller. Bartleman hadn't the reach. And Bartleman had been asked, most politely, to mind his own business. If he, Nicholas Kemp, had been Bartleman, he'd have been well content to sheer off and leave the Marshalsea monster to his lawful prey—N. Kemp.

But Bartleman owned a different soul, and altogether outside of Nicholas's dreaming. He continued to watch the Marshalsea man round and round, while the convicts pushed and clanked for a better view.

The Marshalsea man's eyes were glittering sharply. Of a sudden, Nicholas divined there was fear in them. He felt weirdly sorry for him—even though he himself was the alarmed object of the man's rage. He understood his plight. Unluckily, he must have set himself up among his own company as something of a leader, a hero even, a man of iron, a man not to be trifled with. He could not afford to be as discreet with Bartleman as, maybe, he'd have liked. He must needs be formidable. He had no choice, now.

'I said I got no quarrel with you, mister,' he repeated fiercely. 'My quarrel's with that thieving runt yonder.'

There being no mistaking who was meant, Nicholas groaned and made to stand up—not, as the saying goes, meaning to sell his life dearly, but wondering how best he might haggle to keep it. After all, he'd not stolen the pipe—Bartleman had prigged it. Bartleman had—

'Sit down, son. No call to stand when I'm standing for you.'

Bartleman's wide back was towards him. His coat had a dim shine. The seam had done good service, but was plainly ready for retirement. Over his shoulder, peering for Nicholas, stretched the shaggy, uneasy head of the Marshalsea man.

Then, of a disagreeable sudden, Bartleman seemed to weary of defending the wretched Nicholas. He bowed aside with: 'Here, son, gentleman wants a word with you. I should be quick about it if I was you!'

Whether the Marshalsea man came on at once, or whether he was helped by Bartleman, was hard to say. There was too much of deftness and speed in the embezzler's movements to be sure. The Marshalsea man lumbered past him with a distressing grunt.

Such was his strength and determination, that he got as far as Nicholas and even managed to seize hold of the offending pipe before the neat hole in his side let out the last of his life's blood. Bartleman had done for him as he passed.

'I told you to be quick about it,' said Bartleman, wiping his knife on his sleeve. 'Now you'll never hear that word he wanted.'

But Nicholas had already heard it, breathed out on the man's escaping soul.

'You stinking little fool—' he'd sighed.

This incident, which, while it lasted, seemed to cast a queer glare of its own, ended rapidly in furtive, grunting shadows.

Bartleman, who was possessed of unusual strength, lifted the ragged dead man (whose name had been Dorman or Gorman—no one knew for certain) and bundled him up to a gun port.

Two men hastened to assist—but there was no need. The Marshalsea man was gone horrible quick, and the splash of him followed briefly on—a yard, maybe, aft of the portage that had served for a graveside.

No word of this abrupt and fearful diminishing reached the upper deck. What with the continual flying out of all manner of rubbish, and the intolerable confusion in the convicts' hold, the loss of a soul could not possibly have been known save by peachment. And there was no man there who'd peach on Bartleman.

There was something shrewdly devilish about the embezzler, something quick and to the point that made the notion of informing on him a dream to turn a man's blood to ice.

But there was also admiration. Transportable crimes being, by and large, piddling matters of vagrancy, sneak-thieving, perjury, and the fag-ends of coining, murder flew up like a scarlet banner, and Bartleman stood suddenly forth as a prince of felons, a Captain in the army of sin.

This admiration showed itself chiefly in a general eagerness to refer private quarrels to the embezzler for his just decision. He had shown himself a man quick to take up arms for the oppressed and the weak; and it was wonderful how many discovered themselves to be weak and oppressed when there was a champion in sight.

It was generally agreed that the dead man had asked for what he had got and no blame could be attached to his obliger. The cause had been virtuous, and the execution without malice and commendably prompt.

Nicholas Kemp regarded his strange protector with the most remarkable mixture of feelings ever stirred into a mortal soul. The chief of these was terror, with a seasoning of awe, some pride, a pinch of conceit at having been chosen, a dash of honest bewilderment as to why, and, small but strong, a twist of guilt that a man had died on his account.

This last he could not rid himself of, and the taste of it—together with the Marshalsea man's last words which had been more pitying than bitter—lingered long. Then, little by little, his thoughts changed back into dreams, and his dreams were, as ever, the old wistful memories of the sweet but far-off ladies to each of whom he had given his heart. Truly, never was the nature of a transported felon as blindly gentle as Nicholas Kemp's.

On the fourth day out—the convicts seeming quiet and genteel—the captain ordered all leg-irons to be removed and stored in a compartment directly aft. He was well pleased to afford this touch of humanity, and considered himself blessed with a peaceable cargo. Most marvellously, the quarrelsome parties in the dark of the lower gun deck were subdued. He put it down to the motion of the sea which, to him, was as gentle as the rocking of a crib.

He did not know that, from many snapping beasts, the convicts had been compounded into one, a corporate monster with a host of hands and a single heart.

Bartleman the embezzler of money had advanced himself. He had become an embezzler of souls.

CHAPTER THREE

The captain of the *Phoenix* was a merciful man. On Wednesday, January the twenty-eighth, in the morning, the convicts from the lower gun deck were suffered to come up on a portion of the main-deck, between the forecastle and a roped barrier midway to the mainmast. For three days now, they had been out of irons and as quiet and decent as mice. There was no reason to suppose they'd take more advantage of the open air than God had intended: viz. to breathe it peaceably and keep in health.

None the less, the Captain confided his humane intention to his paying passengers the night before and promised stern precautions against the molesting of young females—of whom three were amiable and one was charming, a Miss Caroline Warboys.

'Even so,' he went on, glancing sharpishly to Miss Warboys, 'I would be obliged if you would maintain a discreet distance from the barrier. Please to remember there are many pickpockets among my convicts; some are most likely diseased—and all of 'em whiff like nine o'clock! So I begs of you, gentlemen and chiefly you soft ladies, don't let your milky kindness get the better of your good sense.'

Here he looked particularly hard at Miss Warboys who glanced down as if innocent that her pert prettiness had turned the heads of the ship's crew so far about that they scarce knew larboard from starboard. So plentiful was her milky kindness that she could not forbear from flashing her smiles at any gentleman in range of them. (It was said that, on a clear day, her smile could rake the ship from stem to stern.)

The morning proved handsome though cold. A brisk
breeze blew across the deck, swelling out the mainsail in
its larboard cheek like a giant's toothache. But the sea was
easy and the *Phoenix* scissored away, turning the waters
back from her bows in high silver folds, while behind, her
busy stern made lace of it.

At ten o'clock the captain glanced approvingly to
the shrouds, where six of his sailors were fixed with
muskets levelled down on the space the convicts were to
occupy. Miss Warboys also looked up and smiled—
thereby causing one of the sailors to slip and nearly
hang himself in an effort to strike a more remarkable
attitude.

'Open up that hatch!' called the captain.

'Open up that bleeding hatch!' repeated the boatswain.
'Open it up and let them poor stinking felons out!'
Then—'Godalmighty what a nose-full!'

This last as the hatch was slid back and the air grew
hazy with the rising heat.

One by one, the convicts came up. They were dark
and filthy. They shrank from the wind; sought to hide
their heads in their scanty coats till they looked like a
congregation of hunchbacks. They scowled blackly against
the sunlight which was harsh and strange to them.

One by one they continued to come, till the space
allotted was almost filled. At last no more of them came.
The boatswain had counted eighty-one. He shrugged his
shoulders. Two and eighty there should have been, but he
was not confident enough in his arithmetic to remark on
it. Two must have come up together, he decided . . . and
went about his business, leaving the gaping passengers to
be fascinated, shocked, and entertained by the sight of the
felons taking the air.

Little by little, as they grew accustomed to the light,
the convicts' frowns diminished; and, as the wind's edge
blunted to them, they began to hold up their heads like a

field of shaggy blossoms, much blasted by foul weather
yet hopeful of the sun.

The passengers, who had shrunk back at the first
emerging, now plucked up their courage, plucked out
their pocket handkerchiefs (which they held to their noses)
and moved nearer the barrier. And the convicts jostled
and grinned and tossed them strong pleasantries for the
joy of making the ladies blush.

One man in particular was doing remarkably well at
this sport, scarleting cheeks like a field of poppies with
language as ripe as old fish . . .

'Enough of that!' snapped a squat, square-faced convict
who seemed to escape jostling more easily than most. He
moved forward and now, with broad, powerful hands,
pushed two surprised female passengers farther off the
ropes—as if for their own benefit.

The foul-mouthed one looked sharply round, then
stopped like he'd been cut off with a knife.

'Sorry, Mr Bartleman, sir. 'Twas only a game . . .
sorry, sir—'

Miss Warboys flashed one of her pertest smiles at
this squat convict who seemed to be exceptional. But,
either he missed it entirely, or he was cased in stouter
armour than ever she'd come upon before. Rather
the sailors in the shrouds, the captain on the quarter-
deck, and the general furnishing of the ship itself
seemed to take him more than Miss Warboys'
brightest smile.

It had not been altogether wasted, however. Someone
else had been hit. A friend, follower, or acquaintance of
this squat convict. A young—a pitifully young—man
with a week-old beard that fringed his pleasant face like
gooseberry fluff.

He caught her eye, paled, seemed to tremble—then
went most gratifyingly red. He smiled hopefully—and
she, being kind, smiled back.

Had there not been so close a press, she'd have been
further pleased to see his knees shaking with excitement.

Unlikely as was the time and the place, Nicholas
Kemp's chief weakness had found him out once more. A
pretty face had so bewitched him that, had the sun been a
pendant, he'd have stolen it for Miss Warboys and let the
world go hang in the dark.

Being female (and Miss Warboys was as female a lass
as ever tipped a hoop), she was the lass for him. Even the
terrible Bartleman straightway took a second place in his
thoughts, and all things seemed temporary till he should
see her more.

During that evening and night his situation among the
convicts—which, on account of Bartleman's friendship,
stood high—helped him make some improvements to his
appearance. He obtained the interest of a one-time barber
who'd kept some tools of his trade.

Bartleman looked on indulgently while Nicholas's hair
was being trimmed and his face scraped over.

'I take it it's for the doxy with the roving eye,' he said
with contemptuous good humour.

Nicholas nodded ('Nearly lorst an ear, mister,' muttered
the barber, twitching with fright.)

'She's a sharp pennyworth, sonny. Too sharp for you.'

'What d'you mean?' asked Nicholas, peevish and
offended on Miss Warboys' behalf. Though he feared
Bartleman to the bottom of his soul, his chief weakness
gave him a certain strength; which strength his three kind
friends had sometimes remarked on. To the barber's
surprise, the meek Master Kemp had the foolhardiness to
frown at the murderous embezzler.

But more surprising still, Bartleman only grinned and
ruffled Nick's hair almost apologetically.

'No offence, sonny. No call for fury. Save it for the
red-haired pussy. 'Twill impress her no end. But then
what?' He chuckled. 'Shall you offer her your heart? Hm!

She's made of shrewder stuff than that! I'm afraid you'll have to do better. Tell you what—offer her this alongside of your heart . . . and then maybe you've got a chance! Here—take it, son! It's going begging!'

The extraordinary Bartleman was holding out a brooch—a charming golden key, set with garnet and pearl.

'Not worth a king's ransom, maybe—but doxies come a bit cheaper, you know. Take it, I say!'

Helplessly, Nicholas reached up—for there was suddenly a glitter of anger in Bartleman's eyes. Was it that the brooch meant more to him than he was willing to say, and under no circumstances would he endure a refusal of it? Nicholas took the brooch—and pricked himself lightly on its pin. Vaguely, he felt he'd taken a deposit on his soul.

The next day proved wild and blowy and not at all prosperous for courting. The convicts only staggered up on deck to be rid of the formidable clanking of their leg-irons which strained at their securings behind the bulkhead: a loud and fearful sound that seemed to beat inside their very heads.

Of passengers, only the hardiest were visible. Miss Warboys was not among *them*. But her absence served only to increase Nicholas's fondness and diminish his doubts concerning the brooch. He was now in the second stage of love at first sight, which commonly took the form, with him, of advertising his heart on walls, trees, and doors. Which aching part of him he engraved on the deckboards, with the pin of Bartleman's brooch.

So it was on the Friday, then, with the weather fair and the sea taking a high polish from the sun, that Nicholas Kemp caught Miss Warboys' eye for the second time.

Still in genial mood, Bartleman had eased his young friend's passage to the rope. Here Nicholas stood for close on twenty minutes while the passengers came out of the poop to consider the morning. Then he was rewarded.

Last of all, and as demure as was possible, in scarlet cloak and yellow wind-bonnet, came Miss Warboys, tripping neatly down the companionway with a glint of silken ankles and a general air of curtsying to the world for its attention.

'Trollop!' remarked one of the female passengers; but Miss Warboys did not choose to hear.

Instead, she glanced up to the shrouds—where the watchful sailors hung—to the poop where the captain walked with his officers, to the great foresail upon which the vague shadow of the main topsail lay like the ghost of a first intention, to the sky—to the sea—to their hazy joining; in short, she looked everywhere but to the young convict whose eyes ate up the distance between him and her.

And *then* her eyes lighted on him—and lighted *in* him such a fire that its glow reached clean across the chilly deck till her cheeks rosied over like wine on a napkin.

'Well might she blush!' remarked another female passenger. 'The brassy minx!'

But though scarce fifteen yards separated Miss Warboys from Nicholas Kemp, so disparate were their situations that it might have been fifteen miles . . . or five hundred, even . . .

In vain the young man stared—with eyes grown huge with longing. Miss Warboys could but smile (albeit wistfully, for the young convict moved her more than she had bargained for) and gently shook her head. There could be no commerce between a lady and a convict save by looking.

But there was no dousing the light in the young man's face. Nicholas Kemp had gone directly into his third stage of love at first sight, which was pretty nearly mortal. It was the stage in which he'd have plunged into the sea for her, gone through fire for her, fought off venomous monsters for her—had she but raised her little finger.

Somewhat sadly, Miss Warboys looked down. There was a distant gleam in her eyes, as if, had the young man not been a convict, her little finger would have gone up like a flag-pole. Again, she shook her head. The lady and the convict were never meant to meet.

There must be a place where heaven abuts on to hell, where angels and the damned may look deep into one another's eyes and say, 'There, but for the Grace of God, might be I.' Miss Warboys bit her lip, then raised her hand to hide it. If only the young man would bid her good morning in a genteel fashion—or even bow—then they might become acquainted. If only he would stop staring at her so mournfully with eyes that declared—for all the world to see—'I love you and will love you till I die.' If only—

If only, thought Nicholas, she would nod or bid me good morning. If only something remarkable would happen. If only—

In his tender extremity, he had wafted out his hand as if to summon up a miracle from somewhere. It was the hand in which he'd been holding his pipe. Unluckily it caught against the rope. The pipe dropped. It fell maybe a yard beyond the rope. It was out of his reach. A kindly passenger made to help . . . but was forestalled.

A swift rustling passed him by and a smell of roses was briefly on the air.

'That forward hussy!' remarked a third female passenger. '*She* didn't need much invitation!'

Miss Warboys never heard her. Having picked up the young convict's pipe, she gave it to him—and with it her hand, which he held with some determination.

'My name is Nicholas Kemp—Nicholas Kemp,' he said very rapidly, as if he'd brought the good news a great distance and was anxious to deliver it. 'From Preston in Sussex. Nicholas Kemp—'

'Caroline Warboys,' said she, with the chief weight on Caroline.

(Though she spoke soft, 'Caroline' was taken up by several convicts and tried out humorously.)

'Caroline—'

'Yes, Mr Kemp?'

'No—no! I was going to say it's a sweet name. And suits you well, Miss Warboys.'

'It was on account of the Queen, you know. I was called after the Queen—'

'Queens should be called after you!'

'Neatly spoke, sonny!'

Bartleman had passed by. He'd grinned, as if well pleased with himself. His passage had been brief—but of consequence.

Till he'd come, Nicholas and Miss Warboys had stood, it seemed to them, in some springtime field, or by a gentle river quite overhung with willow in which unusually musical birds were singing—or anywhere, in short, save on the worldly ship with its windy stench and peevish jostlings.

Miss Warboys withdrew her hand from Nicholas's.

'Will you be . . . er . . . long in . . . in Virginia, Mr Kemp?'

'Seven years.'

'Was you very wicked, Mr Kemp?'

Bitterly, he shook his head. The spell had been broke. Gone was the mysterious springtime. He frowned. Miss Warboys did likewise. The wind had somehow got inside of her bonnet. Her cheeks felt chilled. A sharp melancholy invaded her . . . though the exact nature of it was outside of her telling. Now she wondered what she was doing, standing so close to the convict's rope, even with tears in her eyes.

'I hope your pipe wasn't broke, Mr Kemp.'

He said it wasn't.

'If you'll pardon me now, Mr Kemp—I must go back—'

'Will I meet you again?'

'I expect so, Mr Kemp. The ship's a small world. Good morning to you—'

'Miss Warboys!'

'Yes, Mr Kemp?'

'Miss Warboys—please—I beg of you—if you'd do me the honour . . . I'd be happy—so happy—and . . . and there's no one else, I assure you! Please, *please* accept this!'

In last desperation to recapture what he dreaded had been lost, he was holding out Bartleman's brooch.

'It was my . . . my mother's!' he added hopefully.

Miss Warboys looked at it. Saw it was charming. She looked up at Nicholas. Found him even more so. She struggled with herself. She hesitated.

In all justice, vanity had something to do with her decision. In all honesty, greed had something to do with it. But in all truth, affection and even the beginnings of love gave the final push.

'I really shouldn't, Mr Kemp . . . I really oughtn't . . .
But . . . but as you've no one else . . . and . . . and it
was your mother's, and . . . and . . . there, but for the
Grace of God might be any gentleman . . . Indeed, Mr
Kemp, the honour's quite mine, you know!'

She took the brooch and, as she did so, Nicholas briefly
kissed her hand.

So what was Bartleman now? A fallen angel—or a rising
devil? The blood-stained pipe and the brooch. Both had
been the embezzler's gift. Both had helped to bring him
Miss Warboys.

Absently, Nicholas put the pipe in his mouth. His teeth
encountered the deep dents made by the Marshalsea man's
before him. For a moment, he fancied alien thoughts to
be blowing through his mind: thoughts of some fierceness,
such as a stabbed man might have had if he could. ('You
stinking little fool—')

Hurriedly, Nicholas put the pipe away, and with it
much of his disquiet. Very soon he reasoned himself out
of uneasiness over Bartleman, and reflected that the
embezzler had been good to him. To distrust him was
ungrateful. Bartleman had put a sun in his grey sky. And
what a sun!

He turned his thoughts—without much hardship—to
Miss Warboys, and in a happy frame of mind, composed
himself for sleep. It was close on midnight and the convict
hold was quiet. Nicholas sighed, then sighed again, and
slipped away into his mysterious springtime.

This was a great gift of his—to push uneasiness under
a cushion of hope; even to sleep when other men might
well have stayed awake . . .

CHAPTER FOUR

Nicholas Kemp was visited by the sweetest of dreams. He rode a white horse out of darkling woods across wide, spangled fields. And, as he jogged along, his horse's harness jingled cheerfully (which may or may not have been the clinking of the leg-irons in the compartment aft). Then he was in a trim, fair garden where sunshine and the cypresses played chess across the lawn and a fountain splashed musically (which may or may not have been the dark ocean slapping the vessel's sides).

Now he was in an avenue of scarlet and yellow rose trees, walking with Miss Warboys and talking with Miss Warboys, and offering Miss Warboys the keys of his heart. And she, with a rustle of silk and a twinkling of eyes, was declaring, 'I really shouldn't . . . I really oughtn't . . . but seeing as how—'

Then a shadow fell across their path as, from between the trees stepped a squat lackey, looking remarkably like Bartleman, with another key.

'Here, son. Give her this. It's the key of heaven. Take it. It's going begging!'

'Thank 'ee, my man,' said Nick, in his dream. 'Much obliged. Miss Warboys, pray accept this further trifle!'

Miss Warboys' eyes shone with pleasure that was enchanting to behold. The key was charming, set with garnet and pearl.

'Just sign this receipt, sonny. Evidence that I gave it, y'know—'

The lackey held out a pen and paper that he'd produced from nowhere.

'Sign!'

'But there's nothing on the paper—'

'You ain't signed it yet.'

'But where's the ink, my man?'

'Ink, sonny? You sign for this in blood!'

With that, he promptly stuck the pen into Nicholas's finger.

'Sign, son—'

'That hurt! I'm bleeding! Stop it—stop it, I say! It hurt—'

'There's worse to come, Kemp. Worse to come! Get up, you lousy thief! On your feet!'

Voices outside of his dream were shouting in his ear. Hands outside of his dream were dragging him to his feet.

'On your feet, Kemp! Move or, by God, you'll suffer!'

'That hurt! Stop, I say—' cried Nicholas confusedly, for he was still but half-awake and much distracted.

The convicts' hold seemed filled with swinging lanterns and angry faces. Someone had hold of his shoulder with a grip of iron. It was the boatswain.

'The yard-arm for you, my lad! You may have 'scaped Tyburn, but the *Phoenix*'ll finish you off! Move, I say!'

He moved: was dragged up the companionway into the freezing night air. It was but half an hour after midnight.

He was surprised to see the stars and a wedge of the moon shining both aloft and in the sea: a pair of kissing heavens. Yet such was his bewilderment, he knew not which was which.

He'd not the faintest notion of what was afoot, nor of the peril in which he stood.

'So you are Nicholas Kemp,' said the captain, as if he had long been trying to find a face to fit that name.

This was on the quarter-deck. The captain was much muffled and plainly feeling the chill. Though it was of no consequence, Nicholas recalled very clearly the captain muttering to an officer of his, 'No, mister. Cold or no, we'll do it out here. They whiff so strong, y'know, that, take 'em inside and the whole place stinks for a month! Like cats, y'know . . . '

Under the staring moonlight, the *Phoenix* was a silver ship with a silver deck much hacked and slashed with the black shadows flung by the lofty tentage of masts, sails, and shrouds. In and out of these shadows, phantom-like, came more of the ship's officers to gather in a formidable group about the stout little captain.

'Call Miss Warboys,' he said somewhat wearily.

At once into Nicholas's shaking brain came the unlikely hope that the captain was intending to marry them.

But even his extraordinary optimism and unusual capacity for overlooking plain disaster suffered a setback when Miss Warboys appeared.

Her face under its hood was worried and mournful. Nor was it improved by the sight of Nicholas. She scowled and began, quietly, to cry.

'Is this him, Miss Warboys?'

She nodded, and Nicholas's heart began to beat unequally. What had he done?

The captain turned from the lady to the convict.

'You gave her a brooch?'

'Indeed I did, sir. Oh yes, yes—'

'This brooch?'

The captain was holding out the charming trifle that Bartleman had given him.

'That's it, sir! Why—'

But before he could finish speaking, the captain violently told him.

The damnable brooch had been prigged! When, for God's sake? The very first day the convicts had come on deck. A paying passenger had been robbed by the rope. At first she'd said nothing—on account of being ashamed

of ignoring the captain's advice. But then, in the Great
Cabin that very night (not two hours ago), an unpleasant
scene. The paying passenger—a lady of means—had spied
the brooch, her brooch, on Miss Warboys. Called her a
thief. Miss Warboys had gone white as a topsail.
Witnesses—the lady's husband (a man of means), her
daughter, her friends—had all confirmed the brooch's
ownership. Miss Warboys had burst into tears. Swore the
brooch had been a gift. Who from? Nicholas Kemp. And
who was he when he was at home? Here, Miss Warboys
had looked ill. Piteously. Swallowed hard so's her pretty
neck had jumped. A . . . a convict—

The captain ran on a while longer with detail on
damning detail. But Nicholas no longer heard him plainly.
Instead, an old familiar dismay invaded him. Once more,
his need to offer more than he owned had been his
downfall.

Mournfully he heard at last, as in a harsher dream than
ever he'd had before, the captain grate: 'Take him below.
Put him in irons. I'll have him hanged in the morning. So
help me, I will!'

'It's no use crying, miss,' a grim voice declared as he
was dragged away. 'He's had his chance in this world.
Tomorrow, in the clean fresh air, he'll get his chance for
the next. From a rope at the end of that pole up yonder.'

'I ain't crying for him,' came a tearful reply. Then, with
bewildered melancholy, 'I'm crying for myself, sir.'

There was an iron ring bolted to the mainmast where it
sank through the compartment aft of the convicts' hold.
To this ring was fixed four foot of chain—and to this
chain, by his left ankle, was fettered Nicholas Kemp.

For company he had—in this dark place—some half-
dozen busy rats, the two grinding hillocks of leg-irons
(which were lashed to bolt heads in the vessel's ribs on
either side), and his thoughts.

These were of a sombre, frantic cast. They were deep inasmuch as they were low; they were far-reaching inasmuch as they reached far back to the first-love to whom he'd given his heart (and more) . . . then on through many such buds and lovely blossoms to the black-haired beauty of Lewes and now Miss Warboys herself . . . A bouquet of sweet disaster.

For a while he attempted to sing in time to the regular uproar of the lashed irons. But such songs as he knew were all ballads of forsaken love, neglected love, despised love, graveyard love, fruitless love, betrayed love, impossible love, love at death's door—in short, his songs were all of a love that was scarce more prosperous than his own. Did he but know it he was passed beyond the third stage of first-sight love. He was now in its fourth stage, from which there is no turning back and for which not even death is a sure cure; it lingers on in the air . . .

He paused in his singing and listened once more to the solemn grinding of the invisible irons. Between their clankings, he could hear the industrious rats. They seemed to be at dinner. He shuddered to imagine the course. He sat down and attempted to compose himself for sleep. Then considered he had no cause to wish the morning nearer. Yet waking held no profit, either.

His thoughts kept turning back with dismal anger to the three kind friends who'd seen him off at Deal. Seen him off indeed! He saw them now, as he'd seen them so often before—those three well-born young gentlemen— sitting easy in some coffee house, jingling the guineas he'd prigged for them and waiting for more.

'Well done, Nick, old dear!'

'Lord! You're a marvel, Nick!'

'Don't know what we'd do without you, Nick!'

Desolately, he stared into the darkness and wondered who had made the world and why. Where was his mysterious springtime gone? Where were the hopes with

which he'd been born? Where was his birthright of
innocence now? He'd not spent it—and that was for sure.
Yet here he was, Nicholas Kemp, scarce two and twenty, an
outcast and a scapegoat, damned if ever a man was—even
waiting to be hanged. He'd a glum notion that, though
many a naked beggar got into heaven, gentlemen who wore
cravats of rope were most likely directed elsewhere.

Suddenly, the rhythm of the chains was disturbed.
The regular tolling was changed into a rapid clatter.
Likewise, the heaving motion of the ship (which, in the
extreme darkness Nicholas was profoundly sensitive to)
altered to a curious shuddering.

On deck the helmsman struggled with the wheel, for
the *Phoenix* was come upon one of the strong submarine
currents whose presence, in sunlight, proclaims itself in
long, glass-smooth fingers stretched across the rippled sea.
The effect was as if some profound monster was
wrenching at the ship's keel.

The entire passage across this current lasted maybe no
more than seven or eight minutes, but such was the
loudness and violence of the shaking irons that Nicholas
was all but deafened. When it stopped, and the old beating
was resumed, he could hear nothing external for several
minutes, and mistook an urgent knocking for his own
blood banging in his head.

'Sonny! Sonny—are you there? Answer me, boy! It's
Bartleman here! Speak up if you're still alive!'

Amazed out of his misery, Nicholas cried out: 'Is it
you? Is it really you?'

Bartleman laughed, and there was no mistaking the
sound of it.

'It's really me, sonny. Ain't that a fine thing to hear in
the dark?'

'You've no idea, Mr Bartleman! No idea at all how fine
it is! Where are you?'

'Behind the bulkhead, sonny. Had you forgot? We're

all here. Tell this poor, unhappy lad you're all here! Let
him hear your voices!'

Directly came a score of voices, low but thick with
affection, wishing him well and urging him keep in good
heart.

'That's enough!' ordered Bartleman. 'Quiet, now. Time
enough for roaring later. Eh? Eh?'

Nicholas's spirits began to flicker and to rise. If ever
he'd suspected the embezzler's kindness, such suspicions
would now have been truly laid. Fierce and thieving as
was that man, there was a heart in him such as few
possessed. There was some good in the world after all—
be it never so oddly lodged.

'They'll not hang you, sonny.'

'Much thanks for your comfort, Mr Bartleman, but I
think they will.'

'No contradictions, sonny. When Bartleman says they
won't, they won't. For it's not Bartleman alone. There's
eighty downtrodden gentlemen here who say the same.
Ain't that so, gentlemen?'

Came a chorus of agreement—most determined: most
formidable.

'Did you hear that powerful eighty, sonny? Each and
every one of 'em feels it would be right villainous to hang
a gentle, simple soul like you. And will put his feelings
into action—without which, feelings is so much trash!'
(Here, the embezzlers voice took on a cutting edge.)
'D'you take my meaning, sonny?'

'The ship? You'll take over the ship, Mr Bartleman?
D'you mean mutiny, sir?'

Nicholas's spirits began to dive and twist and whirl, as
might a leaf or a fledgling caught in a sudden crosswind.
The sensible part of his mind assured him that Mr
Bartleman was but trying to comfort him in his last hours
by filling them with hope; but another part of his mind
provoked an unnatural excitement.

'Call it what you like, sonny. For my part, I'll call it
the terrible meek in'eriting a little bit of the earth. Or a
rising up, sonny, on be'alf of you. Or, if you like, a
rightchus anger for the poor little bleeding oppressed.
Take your pick, son—it's six of one and 'alf a dozen of
the other. All that matters is, that you can sleep easy,
sonny. Bartleman's a-watching over you.'

Nicholas did sleep—but not easily. His soul was much
torn with excitement and uneasiness and a gloomy
conviction he'd have no more luck in escaping the
hangman's rope than he'd had in what was gruesomely
known as love.

'Love!' murmured Nicholas, dreamily. 'You've broke
my heart, and now you'll break my neck.'

Then, little by little, his old nature asserted itself and
hope came creeping back. Bartleman, the embezzler—
whose voice he could hear murmuring from time to time
on the other side of the bulkhead—would not let poor
Nick Kemp die. He had promised. Bartleman would—

'Thank you, Mr Bartleman,' he murmured before he
dozed off. 'You are indeed my good angel . . .'

And when he awoke, his eyes were wet with tears.

CHAPTER FIVE

aving nothing of black in her luggage but half a yard of lace of her mother's, Miss Warboys slept badly and woke early, still wondering whether to wear it at her throat or on her hair. But her reddened eyes and stained cheeks—though she would never have declared it—had a deeper cause than vanity over a touch of mourning. Her heart ached: gentle Mr Kemp had stolen more than a brooch . . .

But nothing was ever decided by sighing. The lace became her reddish hair distractingly well—and three pins would hold it if the air proved kind. It all depended on the weather. Anxiously, she rouged the tear stains out of her cheeks and stumbled forth to see how strong the wind blew.

The morning was palely brilliant. The eastern sea seemed to have washed all the blood out of the sun so that it hung over the poop like a glaring ghost.

The air was cold but had little motion. Most likely this was on account of all sails being furled—which gave the ship an open aspect, as of a house suddenly unroofed.

There was no doubt that three pins would secure the black lace quite confidently.

'I must look well for him,' she murmured, clinging to her pertness though her passions were in disarray. 'I must look my—Oh God—God! How horrible!'

From the larboard arm of the mainyard hung a rope that was no part of the rigging.

'Hemp for Kemp, miss,' said the boatswain harshly, then laid his hands behind his back and stared down at the hatch that covered the thief to die.

Though the rope appalled her, she could not forbear from looking at it again and again before she returned to her quarters.

Nor was she alone in this. The merciful captain had seen it with displeasure and even with pain. For he *was* a merciful man—though cursed with a quick temper and a loose tongue. It was certain he regretted the sudden sentence he'd passed in the night. But his word was law to the boatswain; and laws must be kept else they fall into disrepute and are booted aside.

If I weaken now, he thought fiercely, them thieving felons will have the gold out of me passengers' teeth! No! Examples must be made—then we can all rest easy.

'Boatswain!' he shouted from the quarter-deck—and in the general stillness, his voice ranged high and wide. 'I want everything done shipshape! Crew on the forecastle head. Convicts in their enclosures. No passengers near 'em. I'll have no more thievery! They can keep to their cabins or come out with me. Shipshape. D'you understand?'

'Aye, Captain. Shall I read the Service?'

'That's my office, mister. You can dispatch him, but I'll address him. Get moving, mister. And do it neat and decent. Remember—there'll be ladies present.'

The boatswain moved. Put into motion the captain's orders. Eased out the crew from every dozy cranny and dicing hole. Crossed and recrossed the staring deck. A hard and vigilant man.

Sourly the captain watched, then returned to his cabin to ferret out his Bible. On his way, he remembered the paying passengers. He frowned. Had brief hopes of their keeping to the Great Cabin till the . . . unpleasantness was done with.

His hopes were dashed when he saw them, warmly dressed and full of expectation.

'Gentlemen and ladies,' he said irritably. 'I must ask you to keep well aft, poopward, I mean, of the mainmast this morning. An . . . an example is being made. For the convicts. It . . . it really ain't your business. Begging your pardon! It ain't interesting. But, of course, if you insists . . . Gentlemen—I'll trouble you to look to the ladies. Some turns queasy. I recommend aromatic vinegar . . . Miss Warboys! It won't do no good, y'know—not to him nor to you, miss. It wasn't your fault . . . and you won't make it any easier on him. Better for him to think on spiritual matters when . . . Miss Warboys! Bear up, my girl!'

This last, as Miss Warboys tottered and clutched at the table for support. She recovered herself, attempted one of her smiles (which seemed to pluck at her lips like a child begging), then felt for the piece of black lace that lay atop her head.

'Saucy slut!' remarked a female passenger, and Miss Warboys' eyes glittered with a touch of anger.

'Did you see? Did you mark? *That* went home!'

The sun was halfway up the mizzen—a blinding eye to stare the world out of countenance. There was no looking backward towards it.

The masts flung great shadows the length of the deck. These shadows were wide and thick like velvet, and lay most ominously across the hatch that covered up Nicholas Kemp.

'Boatswain!' shouted the captain.

'Sir?'

'All assembled?'

'Aye, sir.'

'Then let up the convicts first. Open up their hatch. Move, man!'

Came a curious effect. The mainmast's shadow lay three-quarters across this hatch, so that the captain shouted a second time before he saw the shabby felons spilling over the edge of the blackness and understood the shadow to be hiding them as they emerged.

Now a slight wind sprang up, coming from the north-west. The flat sea prickled and the *Phoenix* began, very gently, to dance.

'Get 'em moving, mister! Quicker there!'

The captain most likely feared the wind would increase and blow his sermon too early to heaven.

'Move, you stinking felons!' roared the boatswain. 'Else you'll all end up with Kemp!'

But the convicts did not seem to hurry themselves. And, rather than from the angry boatswain, they seemed to take direction from a squat convict who shifted deftly in and out of the mainmast's shadow so that, one moment he was plainly seen, and the next there was nothing but an invisible presence, somewhere in the dark.

'Are they all come up yet?'

'I'll go see, sir. I think—ah!'

The boatswain had gone into the dark, towards the invisible presence.

'What's amiss, there? What are they doing? Boatswain!
Damn you, mister! Answer me or—'

But if that vigilant man had been damned, it was now
by a more powerful Judge than the *Phoenix*'s captain. He
lay in the black shadow, dead of Bartleman's knife.

There followed movement and purpose of uncanny
speed and skill—which the very brilliance of the day
obscured.

Even as a shoal of black perch in a summer's stream
may twist and dart and vanish utterly in the shadows of
overhanging leaves and branches, so the rapid dark figures
of the running convicts vanished in the deep, wide shadow
of the mainmast. Nothing was seen—but there was heard
the terrible sound of their tread, under which the deck
trembled.

Wild confusion had broken out on the forecastle head!
But the man who might have quelled and commanded it
was dead. Muskets were swung and desperately levelled . . .
But against what? Valuable moments lost: moments that
were now beyond price.

Already, this dark and pounding army was swarming
out of its concealment and overrunning the quarter-deck.
Already the captain was overthrown. Muskets shook and
trembled, but the damnable sun glared too bright for a
certain aim. It was too late—and the ruined captain knew
it.

'Don't shoot! For pity's sake, don't shoot, men!
Remember—for God's sake remember, there's ladies
present!'

The embezzler, profiting as he always did by softer
natures than his own, had directed the passengers to be
seized and held in the path of any presumptuous musketry.
His own squat person he shielded with the unlucky Miss
Warboys, holding his stained knife to that trembling side
of her that was most in the captain's view.

'Disarm 'em, friend—or this poor innocent soul dies

for it. Come now, friend—would you want her death at your door?'

He had a way of saying 'innocent' (a favourite word of his), so that it seemed bent in the middle and robbed of meaning.

Wretchedly, the captain stared at the grinning embezzler. There was no mistaking his intent, nor belittling his power to carry it out.

'Throw down them muskets!' he shouted, but his voice was so unsteady with anger, fear, and grief that he had to shout again and again before the crew on the forecastle heard him plain enough to obey. Then several of the convicts ran forward and gathered up the weapons in a triumph they themselves could scarcely believe in.

Maybe five minutes had been needed since they'd come out of their hold and into the iron sunlight for them to possess the ship that had been their prison. To the best and worst of their understanding, they were free!

Five minutes. Each and every one of them had been counted out by Nicholas Kemp. Each sound, each cry, each rumble of feet on the deck had been translated a thousand ways in his eager mind, till there came the shout and roar that Mr Bartleman had promised. They were free! The shadow of death lifted. Any instant now the hatch would be moved and friends would be climbing down.

Convicts were ransacking the passengers' quarters. Bartleman had given them leave. ('Enjoy yourselves, sons!') Roar upon roar of happy triumph declared their finds . . . while the passengers trembled in the verminous grip of felons whose turn was still to come.

'There weren't no harshness—no cruelty—' moaned the captain, more to himself than to the raucous gentry who reeked about his quarter-deck.

Shrieks of laughter rose suddenly out of the poop. A party of mad propriety came falling out. The convicts had got at the passengers' baggage: had decked themselves to the eyeballs in genteel attire. Pantaloons and waistcoats being bespoke, they had sorted out hooped gowns and solemn petticoats; bombazeen bodices and hats like birds of prey. Arm in arm, they hopped and capered, kicking up their feet which emerged from under daintiness like huge black insects uncovered at a garden feast.

In a fatherly fashion, Bartleman watched them, laughed, made jokes, seemed affable, at ease . . . as if with all the time in the world . . .

In the darkness of his gaol, Nicholas Kemp made excuses for the delay. Much had to be accomplished: the crew shut up, the mutiny secured. First things first—and *then* they'd come . . .

On the wild and violent deck, the unlucky captain groaned. 'Why? Why?' over and over—as if the certain death he read in the embezzler's eyes would be eased by knowing the reason for it.

'A good question, friend,' answered Bartleman obligingly. He was in high good humour over the antics of his men which continually diverted him—as if, underneath all his terrible implacability, he was a mass of merriment that could not help breaking through. 'You was going to hang a man—Ha! Look at that!' (Something fresh had amused him. God knew what!) 'A meek, oppressed young soul. So we rose up on his be'alf. Rose up in our wrath. Rage of the downtrodden, you might call it, friend. The anger of the weak and 'elpless, so to speak. Ha! What a sight! Don't it tickle the ribs and warm the heart, friend?' (But the captain's blood stayed cold as ice.) 'You might even say—if you'd a mind to—the poor meek has in'erited this small piece of the earth, friend.

Take your pick. It's six of one or half a dozen of the other. It's all because you was going to hang poor Nick Kemp.'

All this delivered with an affable air over the shoulder of Miss Warboys. On the mention of Nick Kemp, her deathly face took on some faint colour and she began to moan and struggle till Bartleman pricked her side with his knife and made her cry out.

'Kemp?' screamed the captain. 'For Kemp? Then for God's sake, free him! I give in! He's pardoned! You've won your cause! Take him up! All's forgiven! Not a word'll be said hereafter! I promise—on my honour—'

'What was that you said, friend?'

Abruptly, the captain gave up his pleading. All urgency was pricked; all hope sunk. Bleakly he stared in the embezzler's face which was gone suddenly bland. He understood too well that Nicholas Kemp was no more than the martyr whose only purpose was to make the fire burn bright. Bitterly he cursed him for the meekness that had fed this monster's strength.

'Damn you, Kemp! Damn you for unlocking this hell!'

In the darkness below, Nicholas Kemp fancied he heard—above the roar that went with the convicts' liberty—his name called out. Cheerfully he shouted back, 'I'm here, gentlemen! Much thanks for all you've done!' And he stared up to the hatch, with all his amiable young soul fixed on the expectation of its opening any moment now.

On the quarter-deck, one of the ship's officers, in mad and valiant mood, fancied his chances with the squat, vulgar little convict before whom his captain shrank.

'Come along, man. Give up this madness. Kemp won't thank you—'

Still in chains, Nicholas Kemp waited. Then he heard a

scream, and Mr Bartleman shout: 'For Kemp! That was for Kemp!'

What was for him? Another man's life. The scream had a rasp of mortality to it. A sudden and horrible agony invaded the young man, like a blast of winter through his vitals. Into what dark sea had he been led—there to drown? What business had he in the world that men should die for him? He stared up at the hatch, but now with fading hope . . . and even with dread.

The ship began to rock more violently, for the wind was increasing. Nicholas began to be toppled from side to side, to the extent of his chain. Then, with appalling suddenness, a fresh disaster struck.

On deck the ship's motion had brought an almost tipsy gaiety to the convicts. Crazy preparations were afoot for dispatching the passengers—when a frightful sound halted them. Directly, faces grew pale with uneasy questioning, as if the sound was of some supernatural vengeance.

It came from below. It was loud and regular: a formidable rumbling, like fallen thunder, cut off at each extremity by a loud crash. And then there came up, from the same dark place, a frantic cry: 'Help me! Help me! The irons have got loose! I'll be crushed to death!'

'Save him!' shrieked Miss Warboys, careless of the twice-red knife.

But Bartleman, the embezzler, grinned in delight, as if the merriment inside of him had finally burst its bounds. He could scarce contain his laughter in the mounting wind.

'Crushed to death! Poor Kemp!' he roared. 'Now we've sanctified this mutiny in an innocent's blood! We got the right, sons! Oh yes, we got the right! We dedicate this freedom to the soul of poor Nick Kemp! And don't no one go down to fish him out and spoil it!'

Now the wind blew a fierce, malicious blast. But Miss Warboys was long past caring—even though her half yard of lace was whipped from her head and fluttered wildly in the air like a darkened soul taking wing.

CHAPTER SIX

The gnawing of the rats, the violent shaking caused by the passage across the submarine current and now the sudden springing up of the wind, had together broken a securing rope. Thus some dozen leg-irons flew and crashed from side to side with malignant force.

The effect of this, in the extreme darkness, was at once extraordinary and terrible.

If ever a living soul had knowledge of the whirlwinds of hell, then that soul belonged to the young man chained to the mainmast.

With no liberty but that offered by four feet of chain, and no warning of each onslaught save by terrified listening, Nicholas Kemp must needs crouch and leap—he knew not where—as the invisible irons came rushing past.

Sometimes these leaps were too vigorous, and then he was brought down, with painful reminder, by his chain. But not to rest. Even as he lay, conceiving his fettered leg to be broken and his head in ruins, he heard the onslaught begin again. Out of each echoing crash it came—a harsh screaming as the iron rasped across the boards, growing louder and louder and infecting him with desperation to escape, if only for seconds more.

Faintly, from above, he could hear the shouts and sometimes laughter of the convicts who owned the ship. But such sounds no longer moved him. Plainly, from above, he had heard Bartleman shout. He had heard himself contemptuously dedicated to death.

He leaped sideways and felt the wind of something passing. Then he lay still for seconds while Bartleman's words turned in his brain as if that gentle space so full of springtime love and springtime hope was changed into a crucible.

He imagined the squat embezzler standing in the dark, hurling the irons at him—

'I've come for your soul, sonny!'

'Not this time . . . not this time!'

'I've paid for it, sonny, with a pipe!'

'That wasn't for my soul . . . not my soul!'

'I paid for it with the Marshalsea man's life, sonny!'

'That wasn't for my soul—'

'I paid for it with a brooch, sonny, and with a fair face. *That* was for your soul!'

Each of these exchanges marked a thundering past of the irons and a desperate escape from them, though each escape grew more hazardous as the young man tired.

'Not for my soul . . .'

'You took the brooch and bought Miss Warboys' love—'

'I gave—I gave! I bought nothing! I gave her my soul! You can't have it, Bartleman! It's not here! It's not mine! I've beaten you, Bartleman—you've only embezzled yourself!'

'It's too late, sonny, too late!'

Again the irons thundered; again Nicholas leaped— but weariness and deafening confusion caused him to be deceived in the sound. He leaped backward, and it was the mainmast alone that saved him. A most terrific conglomeration of iron struck and lodged against his leg. Though its chief force was spent upon the mast, a stray pendant almost broke his knee.

'Next time your soul, sonny,' the imaginary Bartleman seemed to say. 'Next time, eh?'

Now the 'next time' was on its way, rumbling in the darkness . . .

Nicholas made to move. Demons had been at work

on his knee, most likely with something white hot. But there was worse than that, even. His own chain had been entangled, caught up in the iron. From four feet of liberty, he'd scarce a foot remaining.

He shouted aloud in a rage that was tragic and pitiful; here indeed was the rage of the meek, tricked out of their inheritance and seeking redress in the Court of Heaven. Then the invisible creatures (whose shapes were now, in his mind, grimacing devils and savage beasts) rushed roaring by and met the opposing woodwork with a very doom-laden sound.

He began to feel for the entanglement. Not much time could be left to him. Chain upon chain seemed to meet his frantic fingers. The knot was dense—immovable. He felt farther, heedless of loss of skin and nails. Indeed, the pain seemed to give him a curious courage and strength.

The leg-iron that had struck him was one of the old sort. It consisted, he discovered, of two bars of metal which—in happier circumstances—would be fastened at one extremity to ankles, and at the other, to a chain fixed about the waist. Now one of these bars was lodged between the bolt head in the mast and the linkage of Nicholas's chain. Not even the smith who made them could have devised a more ingenious use nor a stricter hold upon their victim.

The ship tilted and the thundering began again. Above, he heard fresh shouting that marked some new event—or the cheerful expectancy of it. Then the roaring grew deafening as the irons rushed in a different direction.

He believed he felt the air shift hurriedly as they came at him—even as if some living creature had puffed its breath into his face.

'God have mercy on me!' he shrieked—and pulled with such strength and desperation as he never knew he had. Then the irons struck.

For a moment he believed his leg was gone. He cursed and groaned as he flew through the dark, to thump most painfully against a bulkhead.

But he was whole. He was whole and *free* and healthy—or as much so as any man might be, half dead with pain and terror, with four feet of chain fixed to his ankle, and lost in a darkness that was filled with the roaring of loose irons.

When the irons had struck, they had met the entangling bar with extraordinary force; which force, thus invested in leverage, had yielded high profit. It had wrenched the bolt head from the mast. Fetters had freed Nicholas Kemp from fetters.

The murder of the passengers had been delayed by reason of the need to put out a drift-anchor—the sea running high and the *Phoenix* tossing with much distraction.

Four of the crew had accomplished this, either from hopes of saving themselves or from a pride in their calling which would not suffer them to let a ship go down even though they themselves might not live to see her sail.

Yet such was the scene on deck that it might have been better for the sea to engulf it than expose it to the strong light of the sun.

On the quarter-deck, the passengers were kneeling at their prayers, for to each and all of them it had been made abundantly plain that they were not, any of them, long for this world. So they said their prayers, with many a topple sideways as the ship pitched. As they struggled to recover (being quaintly concerned that God might think ill of them if they didn't make the effort), Bartleman would give them a humorous push to see them topple again.

He was in an extraordinarily good humour and seemed

to draw strength from the very air. He could not stop himself from grinning and his breathing sounded like laughter.

Was he mad, then? Hard to say. If compassion, kindness, and humanity are the qualities of sanity, then Bartleman was mad, for he possessed none of them. And, being mad, he had the strength of ten.

'Justice!' he shouted. 'In the name of justice and to the memory of poor Nick Kemp! Heave away, there!'

The unhappy captain stood upon the bulwark below the mainyard. The rope he himself had ordered was fastened round his own neck.

'Heave away!' repeated Bartleman, with a touch of peevishness that the captain wasn't swinging and kicking directly.

But the convicts who'd been awarded the office still failed to heave. Their attention was elsewhere. It was upon a hatch.

Bartleman scowled: terrible sight. But even so the hatch took more attention. Now the crew stared at it; now the passengers rose from their knees. Miss Warboys lifted her head from her hands, and the captain turned, quite forgetful of the strangling rope.

What was there about the hatch that diminished Bartleman? It was moving. It rose . . . and fell . . . then rose again. Monstrous effort from beneath. It groaned, wood against wood, but heavy as stone on stone. It began to slide . . . further and further. Then the deck tilted generously—and the hatch was gone!

A groan of amazement filled the air. A frightful sight was emerging. Slowly and painfully, with much grimacing . . .

Battered about the head, filthy, bleeding, hands and fingers of no more consequence than ragged gloves, even with four feet of chain still hanging to one ankle, rose up Nicholas Kemp.

'Well, sonny!' shouted Bartleman savagely. 'Come back from the dead, have you?'

'Yes,' answered Nicholas. 'I left something behind.'

'Indeed you did?'

'Indeed I did. I left you, Bartleman. I've come back to fetch you.'

By the terror in which he was beheld, it was plain that many thought—for some moments—that Nick Kemp was indeed dead and returned. His emerging was uncanny and his aspect changed as if by passage through the grave. There was almost a supernatural sternness in his eyes, as if he had become the representative of all the meek, the foolish, the obliging, and the gentle whose name and whose cause had ever been taken in vain. In every heart save one, his aspect struck an old familiar chord.

But not in Bartleman's. *He* was never so deceived. Rather was he violently angry at this . . . this spectre at his feast.

'So you want a word with me, sonny?'

Of a sudden, something like his old fears clutched at Nicholas's heart. The embezzler, though squat and with a seemingly short reach, was a compact of venomous deftness and power. He lacked doubt; he lacked gentleness—which two qualities Nicholas owned in full measure.

Confused, Nicholas stared about him. In patches still, the sun was blinding and hurt his eyes. He gazed along the quarter-deck. He saw Miss Warboys who returned his gaze with a smile that, by reason of its very frailty, seemed at that moment to be the strongest thing on earth. It gave him heart, even though, at that moment, heart was not what he chiefly needed. A pistol would have been more to the purpose.

Bartleman had come down. Bartleman was standing three yards off, legs apart, nodding and grinning.

'Can't say I'm not polite, sonny. That word you wanted. I've come to collect it.'

Gently, he swung his knife.

Nicholas began to move. The embezzler watched with interest. The childish simpleton moved somewhat more deftly than he'd have supposed . . . considering he'd to drag his four feet of chain and wrenched-out bolt behind him. Pitiful fellow . . . pitiful . . .

A curious lightness seemed to possess Nicholas. Most likely, this was following on his heavy struggle below. The chain seemed no more than gossamer and followed on like a shadow.

Thus it was almost without interest that he saw the passengers and crew watching him with hope and pity. While the convicts, of a sudden, seemed to him no more fierce or purposeful than sheep on a hillside, watching without understanding while a wolf and a dog were about to fight for their lives. For a moment this thought oppressed him dangerously; then he saw Miss Warboys and at once understood that he had no business to lack interest.

'I'm a-waiting, sonny. I'm a-waiting for you, lad.'

With dismay, Nicholas realized what he was about. It was as if the terrible Bartleman had ordered him . . . for he was circling helplessly—even as the Marshalsea man had done before him.

Wildly, he halted. Bartleman smiled—and took two paces towards him.

'Sorry—but I'm in a trifle of a hurry, sonny.'

Again, Nicholas began to move. Bartleman watched him round. The distance between them was fatally shrunk.

What advantage now in the light of the day? The monsters of the dark had taught him nothing—save the weight and power of iron. And what had he learnt from the dark itself? Nothing—save that the sun was blinding bright.

Where was the sun now? Still over the poop. It had not fallen from the sky. Amazing. It shone with appalling brilliance on Bartleman's face whenever he faced aft, turning his eyes to spots of fire.

But now, with a quickening heart, Nicholas made a discovery no more than a trifle, a feather almost, that came floating down to weight the scales in which his life was cradled. What was this trifle, then? A hurrying in the embezzler's movements whenever he faced aft, and briefly, hereafter, an uncertain slowing down. It was as if he had seen a second Nicholas Kemp, loitering after the first. Then he'd recover himself and resume his relentless watch. Till he faced the sun again . . .

The sun was blinding him, printing false images on his eye! Now, with increasing speed, Nicholas moved about Bartleman—save whenever he passed the poop. And then he dragged almost to a halt.

Implacably, Bartleman kept pace. Even glared monstrously into the very eye of heaven when it was on him . . . so strong of purpose was this man. But his very strength was his weakness—even as Nick Kemp's weakness was now his strength, his heart being neither in his boots nor in his mouth but on the poop-deck with Miss Warboys and out of his present keeping.

Bartleman began to falter—then straightened again. He grinned and followed—with horribly inflamed eyes— followed the image of a Nick Kemp that the sun had burned upon his brain.

So it's possible that he never saw the rush that was made upon him when he faced the poop for the last time. He must have heard it—heard the four feet of chain and wrenched-off bolt clink and bang and dance across the deck; but he moved awry. Seemed to plunge, knife deftly glittering, towards a simpleton made of air. And, meeting no resistance, he began to fall—

'A word!' he cried. 'Best be—'

Then he gave a grunt, such as an ox or a pig might give when its day is done. His fall was finished. He would fall no more, nor would he ever rise.

Like an avenging lash, the iron bolt and chain from Nicholas's ankle had whirled through the air and struck him in the neck. Amazed, the young man turned to look for his enemy. But Bartleman was dead. His neck had been broken like a discarded pipe . . .

The mutiny was ended. The heart and mind of the corporate beast lay ruined before its eyes. For a moment, a profound dismay seized the convicts, then this was changed to wonderment—and then to a strange relief as they saw the ragged and frail young man stare with a kind of startled sadness at what he'd done.

There was a brief and confused notion of offering him the vacant leadership . . . for they were none of them Bartleman. But it was plain that he would not have it. Content he might be to take the fruits of victory—he did not want the tree. Such power as was, of necessity, momentarily his, he used to restore the captain to his office and all else to theirs. True, a few men grumbled, a few men looked askance, a few men even loitered on a violent hope. But there was none of them who'd damn himself to try to catch the universal ear. They were—when all was said and done—more gentlemen of ill fortune than men of ill will. And now a storm of cheerfulness burst over the ship and the shadow of damnation was blown to the winds. The paying passengers dipped into their hearts and gave three cheers for Nicholas Kemp; likewise, the crew. Then, when the echoes had died, the convicts begged leave to try their voices, too. And their cheers were longest and loudest of all, for they knew, better than any, what was demanded of a man to outface the murderous Mr Bartleman.

But what of the hero now? He had been led up upon
the quarter-deck where, despite the powerful smells that
came off him, his back was thumped and his hand was
wrung and every man counted himself honoured to
honour him. He stared at the multitude of faces and heard
the multitude of voices as if in a dream. Then he covered
his face with his hands . . . and when he took them away,
it was plainly seen that he was weeping.

'For God's sake, why?' shouted the captain, thumping
him again and again on the back, as if to give him
something to cry about. 'A prize! A prize! A cash prize,
Master Kemp! That's what you'll get!'

Indeed, the captain seemed to have got cash, prizes,
and Master Kemp on the brain and showed every sign of
staying so demented till his mania should come true. He
was inclined to hop and dance about a good deal, often
twisting his head abruptly—as if to reassure himself the
rope was gone. Then he would scrutinize the shadows—
now shrunk, for the sun was high—nod and gaze upward
to the yards, the fitful sails, the topmasts and the pennants.
On which he'd beam and wipe his brow, as if he'd been
auditing his blessings and found himself to be in credit . . .
when his mania would assert itself again and he'd insist:
'Ten thousand pound, I shouldn't wonder! Value of the
ship! And more! A cash prize, Master Kemp! God save
you!'

Then he bethought himself further. 'And your freedom
as well! I promise! Think of it—freedom and a cash prize,
my boy!'

In vain, the bewildered young man tried to think of
it; but his mind had a mind of its own. Either he'd lost his
wits (as the captain suspected) or he could not help
thinking of other things.

Suddenly, there was a touch on his arm whose very
lightness, in contrast to past powerful honourings, arrested
him. He turned. Beside him stood Miss Warboys.

His knees shook, his heart beat fast and, under the bruises and filth, a blush overspread his face. She smiled somewhat timidly at him, and a female passenger said: 'Ah!'

Wonderingly, he looked down on his battlefield, then back to the lady. Was *she* the cause of his victory? Was it no more than this red-haired young woman whose reddened eyes winked and shone with an ocean of soft tears?

No *more* than? Was it not enough then? Was there anybody on board the *Phoenix* that day who doubted that it was enough? For where else can lie the strength of the gentle and the meek save in love?

'A favour, Captain,' murmured Nicholas uncertainly. 'Might I beg a favour, sir?'

'A favour?' declared the captain, astonished to the world. 'He begs a favour? Freedom and a cash prize, my boy! Don't you understand? It's all yours!' (He paused to glance reassuringly into the shadows.) 'All right—what's the favour, then? Out with it! A hundred pounds in advance? Ha-ha! We can manage. It's yours!'

Suddenly, he observed Nicholas's arm clasping Miss Warboys about the waist. He smiled; he beamed; he began to laugh and rub his hands together.

'Me Bible!' he cried. 'Me Good Book! I knew there'd be a use for it. I take it you want me to exercise me office, Master Kemp?'

Vigorously, Nicholas Kemp nodded. Out of all proportion to the circumstance in hand was his relief that he'd been spared making his own proposal.

She made a charming bride—there on the quarter-deck. It was on the very next morning, which was Sunday, February the first. Two bridesmaids had Caroline Warboys—which was more than she had dreamed of when she set sail. And the tears shed by the female passengers were enough to have floated a longboat.

'Ain't she a picture?' sobbed one. 'The sweet and happy darling!'

In March of the year 1750, the *Phoenix* (now on her last voyage), sailed into the Potomac River in Virginia, with a cargo of hinges for pine furniture, muslins, silks, and thirty convicted felons.

Among these latter were three young men of good families who had been sentenced—at Lewes Assizes—to seven years' transportation for being in possession of stolen property.

On the quay-side they drew a great deal of attention to themselves by loudly protesting that they'd been ill-used, unjustly sentenced, and that money would be coming from England to purchase their bonds.

They continued in this manner for some time, arrogantly ignoring the auctioning of their bonds as if birth and breeding took precedence over Law and Fate.

They fetched very little, being of a worthless and puny appearance . . . somewhat sickly and spotted on the nose and cheeks—as if they'd drunk too many healths for the good of their own.

But appearances can be very deceptive. Indeed, their purchaser got quite a bargain in them, and—despite his being a new owner, having purchased his plantation with a cash prize in the preceding year—was ever after looked up to as a remarkably shrewd judge.

He got seven of the hardest years' work out of those three well-born young men that the settlement could ever remember. They became almost proverbial while they were at it, and often were held up as an example of industry and a desire to atone for their sins.

Be that as it may, their ceaseless labours did much to increase their owner's prosperity, so that there might well have been some truth in the rumour that they'd once been acquainted with him in England.

Had that indeed been so and that there had been some arrears of friendship between them, there's no doubt that they paid off their debt in full. If Trojans had worked as they did, in all weathers, then Troy would never have fallen. Certainly, friendship must have been at the root of it all; for there never was a man so blessed in his friends as dear, amiable Nick Kemp . . .